AARON

But I begin to understand, as the night wears on and we leave more and more bodies behind, that it is not just physical weakness and disease which is killing these boys. They no longer want to go on. They have been cut off from everything that has meaning for them, taken from love into hate, or at best indifference, and they do not wish to continue. They despair and they die. I look numbly on, helpless to do anything but fight my own despair.

ZEV

I don't think I'll kill Aaron, that would only get me shot. No. I'll get him in so much trouble, he'll wish he were dead. Perhaps, just being here, in this room, is enough for the soldier to shoot Aaron and his friends. I hope so. It is his fault I'm here. Him and his stupid father. He has made me suffer. Now I'll have my revenge.

CAROL MATAS is a well-known author whose books include *Daniel's Story*, *Lisa's War*, and *Code Name Kris*. She lives in Winnipeg, Canada, with her husband and two children.

Sworn Enemies

Carol Matas

LAUREL-LEAF
BOOKS

Published by
Dell Publishing
a division of
Bantam Doubleday Dell Publishing Group, Inc.
1540 Broadway
New York, New York 10036

ISBN: 0-440-21900-0

RL: 6.2

Reprinted by arrangement with Bantam Books for Young Readers

Printed in the United States of America

March 1994

10   9   8   7   6   5   4   3   2   1

OPM

For Perry Nodelman, whose criticism I value more than words can express, and for George Szanto, my first teacher.

Acknowledgments

HEARTFELT THANKS TO

Perry Nodelman for his detailed and perceptive critique of the first drafts; Beverly Horowitz for her sensitive editing and penetrating questions; my husband Per Brask for his reading of the manuscript and his helpful comments; Amy Berkower for believing in the book and for quickly finding it a home; Judy Silver for her help in the library research; Shirley Pinsky at the Jewish Public Library in Winnipeg for letting me keep some of the books for a year and a half; Donna Babcock for her typing of the manuscript; Janeen Kobrinsky for her help in many details of the manuscript; Dan Stone for his historical expertise; and finally the Canada Council for their financial support.

Before you begin . . .

Few Jews lived in Russia until the late 1700s. At that time Russia conquered three fifths of Poland, where most of Europe's Jews lived, and Russia suddenly acquired approximately three-quarter of a million Jews. Russia allowed them to remain, but did not allow them to move into the older parts of the Empire, although they could settle in the land more recently acquired. The Jews mostly lived in self-governing villages. By 1850 there were two million Jews in Russia.

Until 1827, military service was rarely required of the Jewish population in Russia. Jews paid specific taxes instead. But Czar Nicholas I decided to change all that. He passed a decree which forced Jewish men to serve in the army. He did not do this in order to grant them the same rights as other citizens. He did this as a move toward assimilation. The czar hoped to reduce the size of the Jewish population and to force Jews to change their religion to Christianity.

The czar's decree of 1827 ordered a specific number of Jews to be drafted at the age of eighteen.

They would serve for twenty-five years, the regular term of service for all Russians. But Jewish boys could be recruited at the age of twelve, in preparation for military service. These children were recruited into the Cantonist battalions, battalions originally created for the children of officers.

The Jewish authorities as part of their government duties were forced to fill the military quotas for both the Cantonist battalions and the regular draft. This became a huge strain on the community, for it was often the poor and unprotected who were chosen by the Jewish authorities. Khappers or captors were hired to kidnap boys when the quota could not be filled any other way.

The religious conversion rates were, in fact, very high and often one hundred percent successful in certain battalions. This was achieved through brutal torture, which the young children could not resist. Many young boys died—some through direct brutality, others by their own hand. The boys were sent to far-off regions, mostly in the eastern provinces including Siberia, where few Jews lived and they were completely cut off from anything and everyone they knew.

Alexander II discontinued the system of forced conscription in 1856, but the suffering of the Jews in Russia unfortunately did not stop with cessation of this brutal policy.

—Carol Matas

CHAPTER 1

Aaron

It was an accident. The first time, that is. After that, it was planned.

It was very early in the morning, just past dawn, and as usual I was on my way to the yeshiva to study. It is a long walk for me, as we live near the center of Odessa in two rooms behind Papa's jewelry store and the yeshiva is in the northern section of the city. There is a very small wood near the yeshiva, and by taking the path through it I can arrive quicker than if I slog through the narrow winding streets of that section of town. Suddenly, right in front of me, hurrying along carrying a big parcel in her arms, was Miriam—my betrothed. We both stopped. I knew I mustn't even look at her— and she quickly dropped her eyes, too. But neither of us seemed inclined to move on. So we stood there, in silence, looking down at the rough dirt beneath our feet. Of course we had never spoken—the match had been made on our behalf by our parents. She was to get the prize student of the shtetle; I would marry into a well-off family who would support me in my ongoing studies. She was the most beautiful young woman I had ever seen. At fifteen, one year younger than I, she is tall and slim with pale skin, black hair (which she allows to peep out of her scarf), and wide, deep brown eyes. My mother was worried I would find Miriam ugly. "She should be plump with rosy cheeks," my mother complained. But I think she is perfect. I worried she would find me ugly. Or too small. Or unsuitable in some way.

A million things ran through my mind as I stood there. What if she didn't approve of the match? Finally she began to move past me. And I blurted out, "You must tell me if you don't want to marry me. I would never want you to be forced into anything."

At this her solemn face lit up and she laughed. Then she looked right at me and said, "I want it very much!" Just like that.

I felt like whooping and skipping like a child! Instead I asked, "Where are you going?"

"I have some soup and bread for the Leskowitch children," she replied. "They've all been sick."

"But you mustn't catch anything!" I objected.

She smiled. "I won't. *You* are much more likely to catch something sitting in those cramped airless quarters, from dawn until after dark, poring over your books sixteen hours every day. I get lots of exercise and fresh air. I'm healthy as a horse."

I had to admit that she was probably right. I knew that what we were doing was strictly forbidden; the rabbis of Warsaw had sent out a decree years ago stressing that young men and women must never be left alone by their elders. But it seemed so harmless. Not wrong, but right.

"Do you often walk this way in the morning?" I asked, looking at the dirt once again.

"At least once a week," she murmured, and then added, "starting now."

I almost laughed out loud. I looked at her and smiled and we said good-bye.

That was two months ago, near the end of summer. Now Yom Kippur has just passed and I am walking to the yeshiva, slowly, for it is Wednesday, the day we always "happen" to meet. During Rosh Hashana and Yom Kippur, when I had to admit my sins to God and repent, these meetings weighed heavily on me. They have been a pure joy but I know we are doing wrong. I asked God for forgiveness and vowed to stop. So I will tell Miriam that we must give up our meetings and wait patiently until we are married. I believe our parents are considering a date around Hanukah, which would mean we have only a few months to wait to be together. If it were longer, I don't think I would have the courage to renounce these visits that have become the highlight of my life. I feel there must be something wrong with me, for I know that only my studies should give me such joy. But Miriam is as stimulating to talk to as many of my classmates, often as stimulating as the rabbi himself. She is far more learned than most women because her father allowed her to study Torah; he and her mother had finally despaired of having a boy after Miriam when three more girls were born. She has a little brother now, but by the time he came along she knew as much as most boys entering the yeshiva. And she still finds time to study whenever she can.

I hear the rustle of her skirt before I see her around the bend in the path. She sees me and smiles. I smile back, but suddenly I feel so sad about telling her we cannot continue to meet. Will she think it a rebuff? Will she be hurt or angry?

Her smile quickly fades, and before I can begin my speech which I have rehearsed over and over again, she speaks.

"Aaron, I'm very worried about you. Don't your parents have relatives they could send you to? Someone out of town?"

"Because of the conscription fever?" I reply, already quite sure what she is referring to. How could I not be aware of it? It is all anyone speaks of. My brother-in-law stood in our small yard two weeks ago, his hand stretched out on a small tree stump, as my mother hacked off two of his fingers with an ax. The Russian army cannot take him now, and my sister can sleep at night finally knowing that he won't be dragged off one day as he walks down the street.

"But I am quite safe," I protest. "A student is exempt—you know that. I have my papers. They would never take a student, especially a yeshiva boy."

I don't say this to brag, but very few are allowed into the yeshiva, and those that are may go on to become rabbis.

Miriam snorts. "I know the decree as well as you do. Students, guild merchants, skilled artisans, farm workers, a single son, the sole support of a family." She recites this with scorn. "In other words, more often than not those who can afford to pay are not drafted and the poor are."

"But, Miriam, if the kahal didn't choose, they themselves would have to go."

"And would we miss them?" she answers. Her disgust for the leaders of our community is obvious.

I suppose my shocked look must register because she then softens her tone. "Listen, Aaron, I know that the kahal is forced to do this by the czar, but the way they have done it in their own self-interest has left me little respect for them. Still," and here she shakes her head impatiently, "that is not my concern. I know the council would *never* send you away. But with this new decree—any man who is to be conscripted can capture someone else and send him in his place."

"But I have papers." I object again.

"You have papers until someone steals them from you!" she declares. "I've heard the army doesn't even ask for papers anymore. Please go now. Just until the quota is filled. Just for a week. Two at the most."

I can see she is genuinely worried. I, on the other hand, am quite relieved because if my parents agree to send me away, I need not tell her of my resolution for another week at least.

"I'll speak to my parents," I agree.

"Fine," she replies, seeming to relax a little. And then she continues briskly, "Now, where were we in our last discussion? Oh, yes. Job. Why does God make us suffer? It seems to me that to say it is to give us a choice between good and evil is altogether too simple."

"Without choice," I remind her, "there is no life, no humanity."

And then I begin to run through the commentaries and to quote the great rabbis who have discussed this portion of the Torah.

We get so caught up in our discussion that the time escapes us, and suddenly I hear someone coming down the path.

Miriam quickly moves past me. "Good-bye, Aaron. I hope I won't see you here next week," she says meaningfully.

"Good-bye," I whisper. "I promise to be careful."

Zev

I just catch a glimpse of a skirt as it snags on a twig around a far-off curve in the path. The owner bends over, grabs at it, and frees herself. It is Miriam. Oh, the lovely Miriam. One day to be mine if my plan works. And here comes Aaron, walking toward me, not a worry on his oh-so-great mind, thinking only about his lovely Miriam. My, my, what a bad boy he is.

Weeks ago when I was walking through the woods here, I heard voices, male and female. Of course that got me interested. I slowed down and made sure they couldn't see me as I crept up on them. And there was Aaron, top student at the yeshiva, the young man rabbis go to in order to discuss difficult passages of the Torah, respected, no, held in awe by everyone in our town, alone, talking to his bride-to-be, Miriam! I couldn't believe my eyes. It is absolutely forbidden, of course, for them to meet alone, and Aaron knows that better than anyone. The hypocrite!

I've always hated him. And this just made it worse. When we were very little, and we all went to the same school, the teacher used to beat me because I couldn't remember anything, couldn't memorize. He used to point at Aaron, little Aaron, who read it once and then knew it by heart. And the teacher would say, "Why can't you be like him?" as he hit me over and over with a thick stick, sometimes on the hands, sometimes on the back. When he was really angry he'd just take his hand and cuff me all around my head. Then I'd go home and my father would beat me too.

Finally, when it was time to go on to a higher level in school, my father realized that his dream of my becoming a scholar (the dream of every Jewish father) was not to be, and he apprenticed me to a butcher. Not a ritual slaughterer, no, not a position that could matter or make me a somebody, no, the lowliest of the low, a butcher. And Aaron's reputation grew and grew, and often at supper my father would repeat some pearl of wisdom that had dropped from Aaron's mouth during a discussion at the synagogue.

But I found myself a more interesting job. True, it's only for a few weeks of each year, but it brings in lots of money. I am a khapper: I kidnap boys for the czar's army.

Czar Nicholas believes he can best convert us Jews by dragging us into the army and forcing us to convert. He knows that by the time a boy is eighteen, the regular age of recruitment, he is too set in his ways to be easily converted. Children, however, are another matter. He has decreed that children from the age of twelve are to be conscripted into his Cantonist battalions. These battalions used to be for the sons of the military, but now they are for Jewish babies. I myself just kidnapped an eight-year-old boy last week. His father, a tailor, died and the boy had no one to protect him. The payoffs to the kahal, the Jewish officials who choose the Jewish recruits, stopped. The boy was mine. His mother ran after me sobbing, pleading, beating me with her fists. I laughed and threw her to the ground. Later that night I snuck into her house and offered him back to her for all her money and the pleasure of her body. She supplied me with both. I gave her back her child.

But now I need someone to go instead of him. I motion to the two huge Russian peasant boys that I've hired to help me.

"Hello, Aaron."

We stop and block his way.

He seems relieved. That's funny. It's a relief to him that it's only Zev, the nobody butcher who has caught him in the woods—who *maybe* saw him or heard him talking to Miriam.

"Oh, don't worry." I smile. "Your secret is safe with me."

He nods uncertainly and begins to walk. We don't move. He looks at us with a question in his eyes.

"Why are we blocking your way?" Enjoying every moment, I want to draw it out. "Well, it must be because we don't want you to go that way."

"Why not?" he asks, all innocent.

"Why not?" I repeat. I can't help but laugh. "Why not. Because the army barracks are the other way."

He still can't figure it out. For someone with a head full of brains he's acting pretty stupid right now.

"And we're taking you there," I add.

A smile flits across Aaron's face. "That's most humorous," he replies. "But please let me by, or I'll be late and the rabbi will be very offended."

"Oh, will he be offended?" I say, mocking him. "Well, that's just too bad. Because as you may or may not know, Aaron, I'm a khapper and you are the boy I need to fill my quota."

Now he finally looks alarmed. "No, that can't be," he exclaims. "The rabbi and the council would never allow you to take me!"

"That's true," I reply, "and that's why I haven't told them."

At this I motion to my two lads to grab him. At the same moment he turns to run, but they are too fast for him. In no time they have him and he is way too weak to escape.

"All that studying," I say, shaking my head, "hasn't given you much strength, has it?"

"Stop it, Zev!" He pauses. "It *is* Zev, isn't it? Zev Lobonsky?"

For a moment I can't speak. Why, the bastard doesn't even know who I am!! He's practically forgotten me. Mr. Nobody. "Yes," I hiss back, "it's Zev Lobonsky." And then I look him in the eyes. "I don't think you'll forget my name again!"

"But why are you doing this?" he cries, trying to struggle in his pathetic way. "Why? Please let me go. If it's money, my family will pay. The rabbi will pay."

"It's *not* money. And I *am* being paid by the council already, to find boys to meet the quota. And you're my last. Oh, I was going to take the little eight-year-old boy of the dead tailor's but his mother, wonderful creature, convinced me to let him be. And you see, by going, you're saving him. That noble thought should keep you happy through your twenty-five years away from dear sweet Miriam. No, I'm wrong. You're sixteen so you must add the years from sixteen to eighteen to the regular twenty-five-year stint—the czar will have you for at least twenty-seven years!"

At this he lunges and really looks as if he'd kill me if he could. When my boys restrain him he starts to scream for help. I'd like to keep tormenting him but I don't want to take the chance that someone will find us.

I stuff a rag into his mouth, which shuts him up, and the boys drag him along behind me to the wagon I have waiting at the end of the dirt road. We cover him with a sack and one of the boys sits on him.

We drive through town, people giving us furtive looks, old ladies spitting, until we reach the barracks. We drag him out of the wagon. As my boys let go of him and hand him over to the czar's soldiers, he straightens and walks unaided. He turns and looks at me over his shoulder. Then he does something I simply can't believe. He winks.

He winks! I should have killed him out there in the forest. I reach for him, my hands out, I will kill him, but the boys hold me back.

The soldiers laugh. "He's ours now, Jew boy."

"Take him then," I say.

I turn slowly and walk away with my friends, slapping them on the back, laughing, showing Aaron how pleased I am with myself. It's been a good day's work.

Aaron

What shall I do? Please, God, what shall I do? I'm scared. I'm so scared. I must not let Zev see it, though. He must never know.

Two soldiers are pulling me toward the army recruiting center. I can hear Zev's laughter. No, he will not have that final triumph over me. I won't let him. I never thought he hated me so much. In fact, I never thought about him at all. To think that he could plot to hurt me, destroy me—it's too terrible. I force myself to turn my head. I look right at him over my shoulder and try to think of something to show him he hasn't defeated me. I'd like to smile but I can't. I manage a wink though, a wink that tells him I'm still in control.

It has the desired effect, more of an effect than I'd intended. He hasn't a brain in his head; he's all crazy mixed-up emotion. He lunges at me as if to kill me but his peasants hold him back. The soldiers laugh.

"He's ours now, Jew boy," they say.

That stings me more than anything. It reminds me that my captor is Jewish. We're used to the Russians hating us, treating us worse than dogs, but our own people?

"Take him then," Zev sneers.

The soldiers drag me into a large room filled with children, the new recruits. They are silent, standing lost and forlorn. Many of them are pious Hasidic Jews and they clutch their peyos—the long soft curls of hair untouched by scissors or blade since they were infants—twisting them, turning them, as if that motion will somehow save them from what is ahead.

I look at their faces, their little bodies, and I realize that I must be the oldest. Most look like they are twelve, thirteen, and there are two pathetic little figures who couldn't be more than eight or nine. Do I know any of them? I look closer. No, I don't think so. Of course, they will all be from poor families, like Zev's, who live on the outskirts of town and go to different schools and different synagogues.

Zev only went to our school because he lives with his mother's sister during the week. Her husband, Zev's uncle, had died years ago, so Zev stayed with them to help with chores in return for food and board. It worked out well for everyone as his parents are very poor and could hardly feed a family of six. Zev's father is a learned man and he'd hoped Zev would follow in his footsteps.

One of the soldiers begins to speak in Russian. "There is a pond next to this building," he shouts. "You will all go out there, undress, and bathe. Then we will give you army clothes. Follow me."

No one moves.

Of course none of them understands Russian. They speak only Yiddish. Since my father is a jeweler and runs a shop which has both a Jewish and non-Jewish clientele, he had to learn to speak Russian. I, too, learned because I often help in the store. Also, he subscribes to a weekly Russian newspaper, and I read that every week. Many in our neighborhood view him with suspicion because of this subscription, but they all crowd around him when the paper arrives and count on him to relate the news to them.

I wonder whether I should let on that I understand. My head is swimming and I find it hard to think straight. Surely there must be a way for me to escape. Surely my life, my marriage, my studies, surely everything will not end here. Like this.

The soldier tries to mime what to do. He points to the door. He pretends to take off his greatcoat.

It is late autumn and the air is cool now. I don't look forward to this little swim.

It occurs to me that if I wait until he becomes really frustrated, I can then help him. Perhaps that will give me an advantage with him. He looks to be my father's age, and by the way he talks and moves he has probably been a soldier all his life, a sergeant, I think, if I read the epaulets on his uniform correctly.

He is getting angry now. He goes to the door and opens it, screaming orders at the children.

Still they remain motionless, frozen in fear and disbelief.

I have been standing by the wall, now I step forward. I speak to them in Yiddish. "You must follow him. We are to remove our clothes, bathe in the pond, and then be given new clothes."

A wail rises from the group. They clutch their talis kotons, the small woolen vest worn under their clothes, and stroke the long blue threads attached to it, worn so they peek out from under their shirts. Will they have to part with them? Involuntarily I find I am doing the same thing. The little Hasids are also pulling on their peyos. Of course they know what is in store for them. Everyone has seen the new recruits being marched through the town. None of them have peyos. Their hair is shorn.

The soldier looks at me with approval. "Things will be much easier with you around." He grins. He has two top teeth missing right in the front of his mouth. Others are half rotted away.

I take the lead and the children follow me outdoors. We trail behind the sergeant until we reach a small filthy pond. It is filled with dead leaves, branches, and scum.

"Undress and pile your clothes here," the sergeant

orders. His fellow soldier, a blond private, just looks on with a small smile on his face. Something about him makes my skin crawl, and I try to position myself well away from his small slit eyes.

I take off most of my clothes and put them on the ground. It is one of the hardest things I've ever had to do in my life. The soldiers stare at me, the other children stare at me. I am humiliated and I can feel my cheeks burning. I go to take off my boots, my new soft leather boots, and it occurs to me that I can't afford to give them up. I know we'll be forced to march and I know how important the boots will be. I surprise myself—I realize I am suddenly starting to think clearly despite the nightmare quality of these events. I suppose I have no choice if I want to survive.

I sidle over to the sergeant, my boots, underwear, and talis koton still on.

"Sir," I say, "I will be happy to assist you with these children. I ask only one thing."

He bursts out laughing. "This is the army," he roars. "You ask for nothing."

"My boots," I say. "Please let me keep my boots."

"Well," he considers, looking at them, "I'll think about it. But see if you can get those brats moving."

Some of the children are undressed but others refuse to remove the yarmulkes from their heads or their talis kotons.

"You must do as you are told," I tell them. "There is no escape for any of us. We must obey."

I remove my underwear, my talis koton, and my boots and I jump into the water.

It is very cold and very dirty. I immerse myself, come up spluttering, and scramble out. I think of the hot baths my mother makes for me at home, of the steam baths I would go to every Friday before Shabbes, and how fresh and clean they made me feel. I am covered in slime, and dead leaves stick to my body. This is a reverse cleansing, an immersion that makes me dirty, accentuates my humiliation.

Finally the others follow my example. I can't help but give one last glance at my clothes. I will miss them. And especially my talis koton. I had always taken it for granted but now I feel such anger. God had ordered us to wear it and now these Russian masters order us to forget it. They have no right!

I follow the blond soldier through a side door of the building. I see he is carrying my boots.

"Over there," he orders, throwing my boots at me.

I catch the boots, then turn to look at the pile of clothes stacked on the floor. Regulation army gear: pants, a coarse shirt, a huge greatcoat, and boots—all men's sizes. I am small, only five foot nine inches, and I know they will swim on me. I try to find clothes as small as possible. The guard motions for me to put the greatcoat on. It is so heavy. How will the little ones survive with this weight on their backs?

Soon they are all in the room, grabbing for clothes in an effort to keep warm.

"Follow me," yells the sergeant. "You and two others." He takes us down a long hallway to a room with three chairs. Behind the chairs stand three men, scissors and razors in hand.

"Sit," the sergeant commands. "Put your coats on the floor."

I am glad to take the weight off and let it drop to the floor. Then I sit in the chair.

I have brought the two youngest boys with me, hoping that, whatever is to happen, I can make it easier for them. They are both Hasids. They stand in the middle of the room, lost in the bulk of their huge coats, and they catch desperately at their peyos. The long soft locks twist and twirl in their hands, one black and one blond.

They'll never survive this, I think to myself. They'll die of heartbreak. As for losing my hair and my talis koton, I know it will feel strange but it is not important of itself. I wear no peyos and the clothes are not what make me Jewish. I know that. But do these children?

Gently I remove their coats and seat them in the chairs. I whisper to them, "It's only hair. God will forgive you. He wants you to live. You must forgive yourselves."

They sit quietly then, but I notice tears slowly trickling down their cheeks. The barber leaves the peyos until the last and then in two quick snips they are gone. I barely notice what is being done to me but I am shocked when I look in the glass. I hardly seem like the same person.

We put our coats back on and return to the other room. As we enter, the other boys gasp in horror.

"It's not so bad." I try to encourage them. "It's just hair." Probably the least of the horrors we will have to endure, I think to myself.

I sit on the floor and we all wait until everyone has returned. Many are white-faced, shocked, and they rub their cheeks where the peyos used to be.

"One last thing to do before we can get on our way," the sergeant says to me in Russian. "Tell them we are going to a synagogue where you will swear an oath to Mother Russia."

We are loaded onto a wagon and driven through the town. We are going to a synagogue on the outskirts. I do not know the rabbi there or any of the people. I begin to despair that my family will ever find out what has happened to me.

In my mind I see our home, my mother waiting dinner for me, pacing back and forth, her hand tugging nervously at the scarf she wears to cover her hair; my father sitting by the fire calming her with his voice, assuring her that once again I've stayed late to study, to argue with the rabbi. Finally my father will go to Rabbi Benjamin and ask for me and be told that I had never arrived. I see the first look of worry on his face. He will go from house to house, friend to friend, call on my sisters and their husbands until everyone is looking—but they will not find me. I think of my mother, always busy working, cleaning, organizing, of my father and his beautiful, delicate work—oh, what an artist he is—

of the room where I sleep alone now that all my older sisters are married, of my books, of Rabbi Benjamin. The tears spring into my eyes and I yearn, I yearn for it all.

The wagon stops. We are herded into a small synagogue. Only a rabbi is there. I thought members of the kahal were supposed to be here too, but I suppose it is too painful for them to watch the boys they have condemned to death or exile take their vows. One by one we are led up to the Bimah, and the rabbi recites the oath to us in Yiddish so we understand fully what we are saying. Then we must read it in Hebrew.

The rabbi is an old man, his beard long and white, his eyes teary. I wonder where everyone else is. I thought he was to have the whole rabbinical court with him, and officials from the Russian government, as well as the kahal. I read the text.

In the name of Adonoy the living, omnipotent God of the Israelites, I swear that I desire to serve and shall serve the Russian Emperor and State whenever and however I shall be instructed during my service, in full obedience to the military authorities, as faithfully as would be required for the defense of the laws of the land of Israel. . . . If, by my own weakness or the influence of another, I shall transgress this oath of faithful service, may my soul and that of my entire family be damned perpetually. Amen.

21

The words make me feel like gagging. To blaspheme the Torah and God like this makes me actually sick. For me this is much worse than losing my hair or my clothes.

The other children seem stunned. They recite mechanically, willing themselves not to feel, not to understand.

Finally it is over and we are herded outside, back into the wagon. Dark is falling. I lean over the side of the wagon, desperately searching for a familiar face, anyone who could run to my father, get help. And then I see him. Jacob, a neighbor.

I stand up and yell, "Jacob, Jacob."

He looks around. Then he looks right at me. I can see that in the dim light, with my hair cut and my army coat on, he doesn't recognize me. The wagon is moving right past him in the streets.

"Jacob, it's me, Aaron. You must tell Papa. Zev, it was Zev," I scream. "He captured me!"

The blond soldier knocks me down onto the bottom of the cart. He kicks me in the side with his boot. I've never imagined such pain.

"You've taken your oath, Yid," he snarls. "No one can help you now."

We are taken back to the barracks and ordered to sit at a long table. My stomach is rumbling and I realize how hungry I am. But the smell of food strikes terror into my heart.

A bowl of soup is put in front of me. Beside it is a small piece of black bread and a cup of tea. The soup has meat floating in it.

"Pig," roars the sergeant laughing. "Pig for dinner."

"Eat!" commands the blond soldier.

Now I see how every waking moment will be pure torture for me. How can I eat without washing my hands and saying the prayer? And worse, how could I even dream of eating anything that is not kosher?

What do I do? The soldier is right. I am the czar's now. Would God want me to break the most basic of all His laws, the laws of kashrut? I stare at the treyf food, forbidden, expressly forbidden by God. It is the spirit of the law that is important, Papa would say. But he would never eat pig. Or eat anything that wasn't kosher. There is no bending this law, only breaking it. How much do I give up to survive? I know Papa and Mama would want me to live; if they were here they would say, "Eat." Rabbi Benjamin? I can hear his words: "The law is given for man and not man for the law. The law is to live with and not to die for!" And I think of the teaching of the rabbis—one may do anything at all to preserve life if there is mortal danger, outside of three things and these are forbidden even if one might die. These three things are bloodshed, immorality, and conversion. If I don't eat I will weaken and die. Perhaps that would be best. No, I cannot give up now. So soon. Perhaps I will be rescued. Perhaps I can escape. I think of Miriam. She would never forgive me if I gave up so easily. And God? What does He want? Is it His will I am here, taking this test?

I look at the other children. Their eyes are pleading with me to do something, to save them from this treyf food.

Slowly I pick up my spoon, I take a sip. I will survive and I will do my best to teach the children to survive also. I take another sip. I try not to throw up. It is horrible beyond belief but I need to eat to be strong and so do they. Otherwise there is no hope. Two of the boys follow my example. The rest lower their eyes to the table. They eat the bread and drink the tea. They no longer look to me for help. They know I cannot help them. My stomach is churning, my eyes are watering. I am just about to let it all come up when I catch the eye of the blond soldier. While he eats, he stares at me, relishing my predicament, so I take a deep breath, look him in the eye, and slurp a big mouthful of soup. He spits on the floor, then gets up and moves away. I put down my spoon, sip my tea, and chew the bread.

I can't help but feel a small spark of hope. Jacob has seen me. By now my father will know. He will go to the kahal; perhaps he will find a way to save me before it is too late.

"Get up!" the blond one shouts. "We march tonight!"

"No!" I exclaim before I can stop myself. "Not tonight!"

He strides over to me and whaps me across the side of the head.

"You dare to question my order!" he shouts.

"You tell your little friends to get up and to move. We are marching tonight!"

I turn to the sergeant. He looks away from me.

"Orders are orders," he says. "The captain wants us to meet up with him by morning. We go now."

And so, hungry, tired, bewildered, the small pathetic troop marches out into the night, through the streets of Odessa, away from home, family, mothers, fathers, all that makes life worth living. My hopes of rescue are dashed. I finally give in to despair, and shuffle, my head throbbing where I was hit, through the blackness with the others. I wonder why God has chosen to punish us in such a terrible way.

And then I wonder if He is punishing me for my wickedness, my violation of all the rules when I met Miriam time after time, even though I knew it was wrong. This thought is so terrible that I stumble and fall against the two little boys who are clinging to me as we walk. They fall over with frightened cries. The blond soldier runs over and strikes them both with his whip. I help them up and take their hands in mine. Yes, I deserve to be punished—but these boys? What harm could they have ever done? The universe I always thought of as full of order, God's order, seems suddenly to be chaos—only chaos.

ZEV

I slept well last night. I made another visit to the widow. She is my first experience in the delights of the body. Actually I didn't think she would give in to me the night before last. I didn't think I had that much power. I figured she would pay me the money but refuse my demand for her body. But I didn't count on her fear, her enormous love for her son. She has a beautiful figure. Her face is nice too, big blue eyes, smooth white skin. She cried, but I didn't care, I liked it when she cried. It gave me even more pleasure. She bit her lip until it bled, but I don't believe she was as upset about it as she pretended to be. I'm as big and as strong as any grown man. Her husband is now dead. She probably enjoyed it but was ashamed to admit such a thing. She is lucky. Her son is safe and Aaron is gone from Odessa forever.

I stretch on my little bed by the stove in the kitchen. Yes, life is good. I am becoming rich. Soon I will have enough money to buy a house, a real house, not a mud hut. I'll let any of my family who want to live with me stay there. Papa is a fool to say he will never touch any of the money I make in this way. Would he rather let the children starve? Well, *they* don't feel the same way. They'll leave Papa and Mama and come live with me, happy to be clothed, fed, and warm.

My job as a khapper is finished for the moment so I'll return to Mordechai the butcher today and continue my apprenticeship. It's boring, but being a khapper only happens once a year—not enough to keep a fellow busy the rest of the time. Although, I have been thinking that I am so good at it, I could travel to other towns and cities and offer my services to the kahals there. Then I can have my own house, and a wife, all the sooner.

"Zev, Zev, are you awake?"

It's my aunt.

"Yes," I reply. I get up, push my bed under the counter, and pull on my clothes. I go into the backyard to fetch wood for the stove.

On the way home from work tonight, I believe I'll stop in at the tavern. I smile. Yes, I believe I will.

Miriam's parents own the tavern, and I know that she will be in the barn milking the cows there because I've watched the house many nights. The wonderful part of this whole business is, she'll have no idea it was me who captured Aaron. Yes, she'll know that Zev Lobonsky is the one, but she's never seen me, never noticed me. I won't tell her my real name. I'll let her grow to love me. Time enough for the truth later, when it no longer matters, when she has forgotten Aaron and learned to love and depend upon me.

All day as I slice up the cows' bodies, I dream of Miriam. I still remember the first time I ever saw her. I was only twelve and had been sent by my mother to fetch my father from the tavern. Miriam was cleaning tables, so modest, so beautiful, her brown eyes soft and full like a small animal's. Whenever I could I would sneak to the tavern just to look at her. And then one day Aaron was there, and I saw them exchange a glance and I knew at once that he possessed my dream. But not for long, I vowed, not forever.

I use the well and bucket behind Mordechai's shop to clean myself up, and I change into the clean clothes I've brought along. I am scrubbed and ready. I walk to the tavern. I go around the back, take a deep breath, then walk into the barn. There she sits, her cheek resting against the warm flank of the cow, her hands moving in a lovely fluid motion, her eyes closed. She is crying.

"Excuse me," I say softly.

Her eyes fly open, full of fear.

"Please," I continue, trying to stop her from screaming for her father, "don't be afraid. I've come to tell you about Aaron."

Her face flushes a deep red and I can see that she

only holds herself from breaking down by a huge effort of will. Oh, yes, she is brave as well as kind.

"What is it?" she asks, her voice only a whisper.

"My name is David, David Lobonsky."

"David Lobonsky." She repeats the name and her face pales. She pauses for a moment as if thinking, then seems to decide something.

"But surely," she says, rising from the stool, "you must know Zev Lobonsky. He is the one who kidnapped Aaron."

"Yes, yes, of course I know him," I answer, drawing closer to her. "He is my cousin. He lives at my house. He told me everything that happened, why he did it—well, I felt that I should come straight to you, because you as Aaron's fiancée, have a right to know."

"Yes," she says, her voice calm, "please tell me what you know. Where is he? What has happened?"

"But first," I caution her, "you must make me a promise."

"What?" she asks.

"Don't tell anyone I've come here. If Zev or my mother finds out I'll be in big trouble. Will you promise?"

"Of course," she replies, sinking back down onto the stool as if she hasn't the strength to stand.

"Well," I say, "Zev knew that Aaron took a short-cut from his house to the yeshiva."

"Many people knew that," Miriam says. And her cheeks get red.

"Well, Zev decided that would make the perfect place to capture him."

"But why?" Miriam asks, and it seems to me she is struggling hard to control her emotions. Still, she shows little. "Why did he want to capture him?"

"Perhaps Aaron isn't as perfect as you think," I answer. "He constantly humiliated Zev at school."

A look of horror crosses Miriam's face. Could she know who I am, what I am up to? I decide to take another approach.

"Well, that's only what Zev told me," I say quickly. "But the real reason is this. Zev was forced to submit the name of an eight-year-old. All other boys had been bought out by their parents. So he met Aaron in the field, away from his family who would never allow him to do this, and Zev begged him to go, willingly, in place of the eight-year-old. Aaron agreed."

"But why Aaron?" she says again. "He could have asked anyone."

"Because," I reply, "he knew him to be honorable."

"If Zev felt so badly for this young boy," Miriam says, her eyes blazing, "why didn't he go himself!"

"Unlike Aaron," I reply, "Zev has to support and help his sister and his family who are very poor. Don't think he enjoys the terrible things he's forced to do. If you saw what effect it has on him, you'd feel sorry for him. I can hear him crying every night as he goes to sleep. Every night. But someone will do the job, won't they? After all, he has been hired by the highest Jewish authorities and the rabbis.

"It is not as if he is a criminal. He desperately needs the money so his family won't starve—he sacrifices his integrity, his good, for the sake of others. How many could you say would have the courage to do that? How many?"

She seems confused now. I am sure it is beginning to work.

"And the final horror for Zev is this," I add. "He knows how you love Aaron. And rather than hurt you he would die himself. Yet he had to put all those thoughts aside in order to save that little eight-year-old child."

"Why does he care about how I feel?" Miriam asks. "He doesn't know me."

"Oh, yes," I answer her. "He has seen you and—and—"

"And?" Miriam asks.

"He loves you," I answer. "He loves you more than life itself. At this moment he is too weak with grief to either eat or sleep."

"But he has sent my Aaron away," Miriam says, her voice thin, her head bent. "Aaron called to Jacob. He shouted that Zev had captured him."

"Yes," I nod, "Zev and Aaron agreed to let everyone believe Aaron had been captured. They felt it would be easier on Aaron's family if they thought

Aaron had been taken by force, had not left of his own free will."

"He couldn't have chosen to go," Miriam objects. "I cannot believe it."

"Aaron feels he can survive, whereas that little boy would have surely died. He couldn't have a life on his conscience."

I shake my head and force a tear down my cheek.

"Zev is heartbroken too," I say. "It has ruined two lives, both his and Aaron's. He loves you so . . ."

"What do you mean," Miriam says, her voice sharp, "he loves me? I don't know him."

"But he has seen you," I say. "He has seen your beauty, your sweetness, your kindness, and he would do anything for you."

She hesitates for a moment. I think I have her. My heart races, everything is going to turn out perfectly!

She stands. "If he would do anything for me," she says, her voice even, "then tell him to bring Aaron back to me. Tell him to go in Aaron's place."

"But can't you forgive him?" I ask. "Can I take no message of comfort to him?"

She seems to be wavering. I can see she is wavering. When she says yes, she forgives Zev, I will tell her my real name, I will beg her to take pity on me, I will profess my love. And slowly, slowly, she will learn to love me, and Aaron will be forgotten.

"Do you not think I know who you are, Zev Lobonsky?" she says suddenly, her voice loud, filled with fire, her eyes burning. "I have only listened to you in the hope of hearing something about Aaron, a hint of where they have taken him, a true story of how you captured him. But I should have known better. All you are fit for is lying and cheating. You love me? Well, I would rather be dead than married to you!" Then she walks straight up to me and spits at me, full in the face. "You are the lowest of the low," she says as she brushes past me.

"Not so fast," I say, catching her arm. "You can't treat me that way. I'll be rich soon. I can make a good life for you. And," I add, now so angry I can barely speak, "if I can't have you with your consent, I can manage it another way!"

I am holding onto her tight. She smells sweet, milk and the fragrance from her own skin mingling in the air between us.

"Papa," she screams. "Papa."

I slap her hard with my free hand, across her face. "Quiet! I'll go. But I'll be back. I'll be back. You have a brother, only six. In two years I can send him. You'd better be nice to me. Think about it. I'll be back."

She's quiet now. I stride to the barn door. I look back. Her hand is on her face.

"I'll be back," I repeat.

Then I hurry away, past the tavern, toward home. My mood is black. She tricked me. She led me on, fooled me completely, knowing all the time who I was. Love, who needs it? It only makes an idiot out of you. But I will have her. If I need to force her, I will have her. She will be an addition to my beautiful home, she will be a possession I can be proud of. She and Aaron will not look down on me any longer. No, he is as good as dead and one day she will be my wife. I will have what I want.

CHAPTER
5

Aaron

My boots will save me. All the others have boots
many sizes too big which makes it almost impossible
for them to walk, let alone march. We have trudged
through the night by the light of the moon and stars,
and now as dawn breaks I think of the harsh truth
of the two bodies that sagged down into the earth
during the march. The two little boys are dead.
They simply lay down and gave their spirits to God.
I stopped and said Kaddish, the prayer for the dead,
over their little bodies, but I could not weep. I could
not weep because it took all my strength not to do
the same thing—I was so tempted to lie down beside
them and never get up.

When I continued on I was overtaken by an emotion I have never before experienced. Hate. Zev's
face looms before my eyes and I know that if he

stood in front of me now I would be capable of killing him with my bare hands. I have lived my life surrounded by love and warmth, I have been sheltered and protected, in my life as a student, I have never known hate. To hate goes against everything I have ever learned. It is true that once or twice I joined the boys in my street as we fought the roughnecks from the poor side of town. And won! But that wasn't hate. This feeling is almost stronger than what I feel for Miriam. And I want revenge. I want to live and pay him back. See him suffer as he's making me suffer. An eye for an eye. Isn't it written in the Torah? He needn't die—unless I do. Otherwise he can suffer as I have. And yet, I can hear my father's voice admonishing me. "We mustn't take the Torah writings too literally. After all, do we offer animal sacrifices in 1851? No. We do not. We interpret the law all the time. We look for the heart of the law, the moral issues, we debate, we think, *then* we act. We are not puppets who do *exactly* as we are told." Revenge would not be within my father's parameters. But perhaps, if it helps me to stay alive, he will forgive me. And then there is love. I cannot wait twenty-seven years to start a normal life, marry, have children, study. I cannot expect Miriam to wait that long for me, so as we march I devise a plan. I shall escape. I don't know how, but I know that I will not spend twenty-seven years in the czar's army. So I will bide my time, and then, somehow, I will escape Russia altogether and start a new life. Perhaps France or England or even America. Who knows?

"There they are," the sergeant calls. Another troop is standing on the road, waiting for us. The officers, like ours, are on horseback. There must be a hundred children. The closer we get the more horrible a sight it becomes.

They are all pale, their eyes sunk deep into their emaciated faces, their huge coats swimming on their skeletal frames. They do not smile or talk. They simply stand, frozen. As we get closer one falls to the ground. A couple of his friends kneel over him. They carry him a few feet into the field and I can hear their voices raised in the mournful song of Kaddish. Why do they fall down and die so easily? Why won't they fight?

We march until the sun is well up in the sky and we finally reach a small town. There we are billeted in a long, low army barracks. We are seated in the dining hall where a vegetable borscht is served. I eat every mouthful. I know it is not kosher, that it has probably all been cooked with lard, but I refuse to die because of that. In fact, I cannot believe God would want me to. I look at the others who are eating only bread and tea. Perhaps, on the other hand, I am wrong and this is a test from God to see how devout I really am. Well, now He knows. It's strange, but I always thought that if I was ever put to the test, I would be like the great martyrs of our faith. Now I find that I would rather live than be pious. In fact, the more I think about everything the angrier I become at God. If He loves us, how can He allow this to happen?

The sergeant's voice abruptly interrupts my thoughts, and for once I am almost glad of a distraction, anything so that I need not think.

"We march to other quarters," he orders. "We will arrive there tonight and remain for a week in order to get done what needs to be done."

We line up in a ragged formation and march through the town. The weather has suddenly turned cold. A heavy cloud cover hangs over us and I can see my breath. I feel that it will snow soon. What did the sergeant mean by that comment? What needs to be done?

We march all day without rest. At least ten of the hundred recruits we joined up with fall by the way-side as we march. I imagine that they have been marching for weeks, they look so thin and misera-ble. And most, of course, are from poor families to begin with so they haven't the strength or the stam-ina to carry on. Many are wracked with terrible coughs, and I can see by the shine in their eyes that they are burning with fever.

But I begin to understand, as the night wears on and we leave more and more bodies behind, that it is not just physical weakness and disease which is killing these boys. They no longer want to go on. They have been cut off from everything that has meaning for them, taken from love into hate, or at best indifference, and they do not wish to continue.

They despair and they die. I look numbly on, helpless to do anything but fight my own despair.

Finally we arrive at a small town of no more than a thousand people. I see candles in some of the windows and with a terrible jolt I suddenly realize it is Friday night. Shabbes. I picture sitting at the table with my mother and father. I can smell all the fresh hallah bread, I can see my mother's pearls gleaming in the candlelight, and my father's face glowing with the pleasure of Shabbes after we return from the baths. And I can see my father and me going to shul the next day where I will argue with the other students and the learned men and, yes, I suppose, be the center of attention. I miss everything so much I feel it as a physical pain in my heart and I feel that my heart will break.

The barracks are on the outskirts of the town, and we are hustled into the long dining area for bowls of pork soup, bread, and tea. Even after the long walk, most will not eat the soup. I do.

After we have eaten we are given a blanket and ushered into a dormitory, with about twenty cots. The room is dimly lit with lamps. To me, it looks like heaven. Can life have changed so fast? I am so tired I almost weep with joy when I see the cots. Everyone hurries to find a place to sleep. We needn't worry though; they only allow twenty of us in, enough beds for all.

We are about to lie down and sink into blissful oblivion when the blond soldier shouts at us from the door, "You will all kneel and pray."

We look around, confused. Jews do not kneel when they pray. And why would they let us pray now?

Two black-robed priests enter the room.

"I will lead the prayers," one of them says, quietly. "We will pray until you are ready to take holy baptism. Once baptized you will rest."

"There will be no rest, no sleep, for any Jew," the soldier laughs, "only for good God-fearing Christians. Now kneel by your beds or you will feel my rod!" He swirls a long heavy rod he is carrying in his hand through the air.

So this is what must be done. My fatigue is so great I feel I cannot fight. To sleep, and therefore to live, I must be baptized.

I feel like screaming, hitting, fighting, going to my death with some dignity, at least. But no, I realize I must not go to my death. I have vowed that I will not give in.

"Fine," I mutter to myself, "I will kneel. And I will use the time to go over the Torah in my mind, so I do not forget. This will be my study period."

I have studied the Torah for so long and so deeply that I can recite most of it by heart. Still, memorizing the words does not mean you understand them. Great scholars spend their entire lives studying one or two sections. And that is what I will do. I will first of all go over it and over it for memory, and then I will initiate discussions with myself. I shall learn. I shall *not* give in. Still, it will be hard to concentrate, and a feeling of terrible dread creeps through me.

I kneel at my cot and begin slowly to rock back and forth as I recite the verses silently. I dare not mutter them aloud, in case they should suspect me.

The priests begin to intone in Russian from the Bible.

Time passes.

Suddenly my back is searing with pain. The soldier stands over me.

"Fall asleep again," he shouts, "and you will have two hits, not one. A hit for every time you doze off!"

I didn't mean to fall asleep. It just happened. I look around. The others look horrible. Eyes glazed with fatigue. One very young boy is passed out, lying down on a cot. Did he give in while I was asleep? Is that why they didn't notice me right away?

I begin to experience a strange floating sensation, as if I am immersed in water. Everything seems unreal, dreamlike. I recite the passages from Genesis, trying to concentrate, making sure I am letter-perfect. I force myself to stay awake.

The boy next to me slumps onto a cot. He must be around twelve years old, although his face and eyes look older. The soldier comes over, lifts his arm high, and brings the rod down on the boy's back with a slap! The boy screams. "I give in," he cries in Yiddish. "I give in."

The priests rush over. They pull the boy out of

the room. Within minutes he returns, a cross hanging from a chain at his neck.

"Sleep now," one of the priests says. "You can sleep in peace. You are a true Christian." The boy falls onto the cot and is asleep in seconds.

I peer at him. It looks easy. So easy. But I keep repeating the Torah passages over and over to myself, fighting the sound of the priest's prayers. Finally I see the priest blow out the lantern because light is filtering into the room from outside. My stomach is screaming for food. The smell of borscht wafts into the room. I've made it through the night and now I will eat to regain my strength.

"Get up," the soldier yells at us. "Get ready to march. No food for any Jew. Food only for the baptized!"

I'm angry and disappointed but mostly I feel helpless—and that is the worst feeling of all. I glance over at the boy sleeping peacefully in the bed beside mine.

The private with no name, the blond menace, stalks over to his cot and strikes him. "Wake up, little brother." He smiles maliciously. "It is a new day!"

I can see we won't be treated much better even if we convert. The soldier, I think, should at least pretend to be nice to the newly converted so he can help convince the rest of us. But perhaps even that is unnecessary. Perhaps they know we will all give in, no matter how badly we are treated.

The boy doesn't stir. The soldier shakes him

harder. Still the boy remains motionless. I finally realize that he is dead. It is so easy to die here. One can just close one's eyes and slip away. There is no struggle, no need to hold on to life, nothing to fight for. Death is easy, someone dear who waits for you with open arms, just like your mother.

I struggle to my feet. My back is screaming with pain, both from the rod and from kneeling for so long. My legs are cramped and my knees feel like one big bruise. Still I welcome the fresh air and the movement.

We are lined up in rows of two, marched into a field, and forced to march back and forth, in rhythm, across the field, all day. We are given no food, no water. The priests hover at the edge of the field. By the end of the day half of the recruits have staggered to the side of the field for their baptism. They are given food and water in front of the rest of us (although some will still only eat bread—a strange kind of conversion) and are then allowed into the barracks to sleep.

The dreamlike quality I experienced as I was kneeling all night is becoming more and more pronounced. My head feels light, as if it is floating above me, and yet my body moves as if weighted down with lead. Nothing seems real anymore. Not this, and not my other reality, the one I left behind. I try to think of Mama and Papa, of my sisters and my brothers-in-law, and of course of Miriam. But none of them seems real, rather more like figures I have conjured up in my dreams.

It is getting dark.

"Bedtime," calls the sergeant who has been marching us up and down the field.

We shuffle into the barracks. I look at my cot. What will I give to be allowed to sleep in it? My soul? My religion? My life?

Hadn't I vowed to survive? Hadn't I promised myself? Shall I keep this up until it's too late and I lose all my strength and I die? But perhaps they will quit. Perhaps they will push us only so far.

"Kneel!" shouts the blond soldier. We stumble to our cots and kneel.

The smell of food seems to envelop me. The food that will keep me strong, keep me alive. But wait, how is it that by breaking kashrus, one of God's most important commandments, I am made stronger? Does that mean it was always meaningless? Just an old rule, from superstitious people, thought up five thousand years ago because pigs were dirty then and caused illness? Is that it? And if that is true, what else is true? Suddenly I have a terrible thought. Is there a God at all? Does He even exist? I almost stop breathing as the thought sinks its tendrils into my brain and heart and moves through me like a grasping organism. Does He exist? I almost faint then but I manage to hold on, to continue to kneel.

Will I die for my faith? Would God want me to? Is there even a God?

I am so confused I don't know what to do. Perhaps God is even now rewarding the little dead martyrs in the world to come. And if I give in, perhaps He will punish me in the next world. Or I could convert, and then die soon, and get no pleasure in this world or the next. My head spins.

I suddenly realize that I do not know and I may never know what God wants. I don't know if God still wants me or if I still want Him. The picture of Miriam forms before me and I realize that I do know about love. Then the picture of Zev forms before me and I also realize that now I know about hate. In fact, I feel this hate so intensely that shame overcomes me with equal intensity and I no longer know anymore who I am, what I am becoming, or even who I really was. If I can feel this hate now, then it was always inside me, was it not? And I was not the gentle, learned scholar I thought I was. Perhaps I don't even *deserve* to live anymore. I'm becoming a monster, filled with rage. I should be able to forgive Zev, to pity him even, but all I want is revenge.

I think of the three major obligations, the focus of our Jewish covenant with God: Torah study, marriage and children, and the mitsvos or good deeds. I can do none of those if I'm dead. And yet I know that there are three things one must not do, even if it is to preserve life—shed the blood of others, behave immorally, and convert. The law seems clear then. I should choose death. But I don't want to! And that is what I suppose I must base my decision on, in the final analysis. I don't want to die. I want to live.

I decide to pray. I say the Sh'ma, the prayer all

Jews say as they die. For now, formally, I will die as a Jew.

Sh'ma yisroayl, Adonoy elohaynu, Adonoy ehod.

Hear O Israel, the Lord our God, the Lord is One.

I push myself to my feet and slowly shuffle over to the priests. It occurs to me that it is Saturday night, the end of the Sabbath, the holiest of days. The thought comes again, "Perhaps, God, You don't exist after all."

ZED

It's time to get ready for the Sabbath. I grab my clean clothes and run out into the street, which is now filling up with men and boys. Everyone is heading for the bathhouse. My cousin Adam is hurrying after me, trying to keep up. His sister Sarah is at home with my aunt Rachel, cleaning the house, putting the final touches on the Shabbes meal. Aunt Rachel is a good cook, better than my mother, and each Shabbes we indulge in chicken soup, hallah, noodles, and fresh fish. During the week she works as a clockmaker, having taken over the business when my uncle died. At first everyone was shocked that she, a woman, could do such a job, but when Uncle Daniel was alive she used to help him at home and he taught her everything. Now people are used to her and she makes a good living.

I like working for her—I do very little and it gets me away from my own house, crammed with people and poverty.

I reach the bathhouse, strip to my underwear, and enter the steam room. The steam is so thick I can't exactly recognize anybody, but there is the familiar thwacking sound as friends gently hit each other on the back with special brooms made of birch twigs. I instruct Adam to do the same for me, and I sit, inhaling the hot moist air, feeling the sharp but sweet crackle of the twigs on my skin.

I wonder what Aaron is doing just now, and I let out a small satisfied laugh.

"That's it," I say to Adam, "keep it up."

"He laughs!" a voice says through the steam.

I peer into the mist but can't make out who the speaker is.

"He laughs," the voice repeats again. "He sends my Aaron off to certain death, and he sits here, among us, as if he could ever be clean, and he laughs. Will my Aaron live? And even if he does, won't I be dead in twenty-seven years? He has killed my child. Does he have the right to sit here among us, laughing? Does he?"

"No, no, he doesn't," other voices join in. "Throw him out! Make him leave. Scum. Villain. Pig."

It is hot, very hot, but I can feel cold chills running up and down my spine. Aaron's father! I should have realized that I might meet him here. What should I do? Better dress quickly and go. I still must immerse myself three times in the mikva. It isn't steamy in that room so I had better leave before Aaron's father does and I really have to face him.

I rise slowly, hoping the steam will help my escape.

I hear the voice again.

"Zev Lobonsky, this is a warning from David Churchinsky, father of Aaron. If I, or any of my friends, find you here or in shul or *anywhere,* and that includes Miriam's barn, we cannot guarantee your continued good health. No, we cannot guarantee it at all." His voice breaks. "I don't care what happens to me now, I have lost my son, so you, you watch out for yourself."

Now I am sweating, the sweat pouring from my body. The room is silent, filled with menace. I can hear Adam beside me, whimpering. I grab his hand and drag him from the steam room. We immerse ourselves three times in the mikva, then change quickly, all under the stony glare of the other men and boys. We hurry out of the bathhouse.

My mind is whirling. Aaron's father sounded serious, deadly serious. He is a small man, a master craftsman with delicate hands, but he is smart and he has lots of friends. Even the kahal might not protect me because they never had Aaron on their list, and in fact Aaron's father had paid them well to keep him off it. Maybe I *should* go to another town and find work as a khapper. And maybe I should do it right away. Well, I can't travel on Shabbes, but I'll leave first thing Sunday morning. Of course I have to go to shul tonight, it is Shabbes and I'm not going to let their threats get me to drop my duties to God. God understands that my work has the full approval of the council and that it is noble of me to do work that others wouldn't touch. However, He may not quite understand why Aaron had to go—still, I saved that little boy. I must go and pray so He can see that I am still pious and devout. I wouldn't want Him to get the wrong idea.

I hurry home, leave my dirty clothes, and start out for shul. Adam, as always on Shabbes, is by my side.

"But, Zev," he says, "aren't you afraid they'll hurt you if you go to shul tonight?"

I laugh. "On Shabbes? Never." Still, I don't think I would venture there on any other morning. "They would never desecrate the Sabbath by violence," I reassure him. "We'll be fine."

At synagogue I have a row completely to myself. No one speaks to me, no one wishes me a good Shabbes. I pray fervently to God, and then when the service is over I walk home with Adam. I sit down to the evening meal, the Shabbes candles gleaming, the house sparkling clean. I am warmed by the heat of the stove, which has been in use all day. I bite into the thick fresh piece of hallah. I think of Aaron and I have to smile. I wonder how he is celebrating Shabbes tonight.

•   •   •

"Zev, Zev, wake up!"

Adam is pushing me.

"Wake up!"

I sit up with a start and stare at him, bewildered. It is very early in the morning, the room is still almost dark. "What is it?" I ask. "Is someone sick, or dead?"

"My friend Daniel came over to tell me," Adam says, "that there's a group of men gathering at the Churchinsky home. They are going to take you to a rabbinical court. They want to put you on trial."

Now I am wide awake. I scramble out of bed, gather my clothes, and shove them into a bundle. I reach under my mattress and feel for my bag of money.

"They're coming," Adam exclaims. "Hurry."

I pull on my pants, boots, shirt, and my winter coat and hat. I kiss Adam. "Thank you, sweetheart. You've saved me from them. Tell your mama what's happened. I'll run out the back door." I can hear them banging on the front door and I race out the back, through the tiny yard and onto the street. I sprint through the back ways, heart thudding, and head for the road out of town. I manage to flag down a traveling salesman who is plodding along with his cart.

"Say, you," I shout, showing him more money than he could hope to make in a month, "let me get in your cart, under the wares, and take me just to the next town."

He nods, takes the money, and I cover myself with bits of cloth, pots, pans, whatever. The time drags by, the horse plods on, and after a while I relax, knowing I've fooled them and gotten away. I make my plans.

Conscription will soon be over for this year so I must try to make as much money as fast as possible. In many towns they are desperate to fill their quotas so as not to get in trouble with the authorities, but they haven't got khappers who really know their business. I know mine. I'll write the town kahal and demand they control Aaron's father. After all, they hired me so they must stick by me. Soon I'll be able to return home.

I must have fallen asleep, for I wake with a start as the wagon pulls up short.

"We're here," the driver says.

I get out, my bundle over my shoulder, and wander into the strange streets of the town. I walk for a while until I find the Jewish section. I look at the shops, the people in the streets. I must ask for the name of the kahal and offer my services as a khapper to them.

I stop a young man who is walking past me. He gives me the name and address of the chief Jewish official, a Mr. Meyer. He then points the way and within minutes I am standing at the door of a large impressive home. I bang the knocker. A maid answers.

"Please," I say, "I have business with the master of the house. May I see him for just a minute?"

She looks me up and down, then frowns. "I'm sorry, sir," she replies, "no one may see Mr. Meyer without an appointment."

I hear a ruckus in the hall behind her.

"Well, what am I to do?" booms a voice. "They're all out hiding in the woods. If I can't find at least one more Jewish boy, I shall have to go myself."

I see a large burly man stalking down the hall, coat and hat on, speaking to a small timid fellow who is hurrying along beside him.

Boldly I step past the maid. "Mr. Meyer, Mr. Meyer," I call.

"Who is this?" the large man demands, glaring at the maid.

"I come in answer to your prayers, Mr. Meyer." I smile. "'I am a khapper from Odessa and I will help you fill your quota."

I see him staring behind me. I turn and see a Russian captain and two burly sergeants walking toward the house.

"Here they come," he wails. "What shall I tell them? They're coming for me!"

"Don't be silly," I say. "I'll find someone for you—for the right price!"

"Fine, fine, boy, let me see your papers."

And then I feel like my heart has stopped. My papers. I can see them clearly, tucked away in the kitchen cabinet where they will be safe. How could I have forgotten my papers?

"M-my papers," I stutter. "Just let me look." I make a show of looking, but I know where they are. "Why," I say, trying to seem completely surprised as I pull at my pockets, "I must have left them in Odessa. I was in a hurry. Never mind. I'll return home, get them, and be back here tomorrow morning."

"But that won't do," Mr. Meyer says, staring at me. "They are coming for someone now. What is your name?"

"Zev. Zev Lobonsky."

The Russians are at the door now.

"We march today, Meyer," the captain declares. "Are you ready to come with us?"

If the kahal cannot find recruits, then the army will take them instead. Mr. Meyer looks around in desperation. The little man shrugs his shoulders and then turns his eyes on me. The man Meyer does the same. When Meyer speaks I am sure, at first, that I have heard him wrong. My Russian is not very good and of course that is what he speaks to the soldiers.

"Captain, Captain, you see we have someone for you. A fine, strong young man, Zev Lobonsky, who is wandering our streets with no papers."

I can't speak. I am too stunned to object. I myself have used this tactic many times because any male found without papers can be immediately conscripted.

I must escape. It is my only hope. I turn and with all my strength try to barrel through the three Russians, but my arms are grabbed and the captain cuffs me across the head.

"What?" he demands. "You do not wish to serve your country?" He hits me again and the pain reverberates through my head.

Suddenly I start to laugh and I can't stop.

"It's a joke," I say, gasping for air. "Just a joke, correct? Don't worry, I'll catch you ten good recruits by tomorrow. I'm a khapper! You can't take me!"

Mr. Meyer and his friend turn back into the house. The maid shuts the door.

"You're ours now, Jew boy," says the captain. And they pull me down the street.

Aaron

For two days now I've had to watch as one by one the boys give in to conversion, their spirits and bodies broken by hunger, thirst, and fatigue. The boy who sleeps next to me is the last of our group to give in. I don't know how he's had the strength to hold out for an extra two days. Finally, though, he staggers to the priests. When he returns with a cross around his neck I can see he wants to die. I recognize that look now. All the life seems to go from the eyes and just a dull stare is left, as if the soul is getting ready to leave the body; the eyes look inward, not outward anymore. I want him to wake up tomorrow morning.

"Samuel," I say to him, as he lies on his cot, "Samuel, listen to me. God would want us to live."

"No," Samuel replies, shaking his head, "He

would want us to die rather than give up our faith. It's just that I am weak and I gave in."

"How do you know that's so?" I ask.

"How do you know it isn't?" he replies.

Well, I don't. I have lain awake wondering whether I have made the right choice. Perhaps I should have held out until I died. I know that suicide is wrong, but is fighting for your deepest beliefs wrong? Then I'd wonder if God exists at all or, if He does, whether I love Him anymore. Perhaps He is cruel and unjust. Perhaps He has chosen us only to make us suffer. Now, however, isn't the time to discuss this with Samuel.

"Tell me about your family," I say.

"I am the youngest of eight," he replies. "My father sells fruits and vegetables in the market. We are very poor. He couldn't afford to buy my freedom. But I have studied," he adds proudly. "I am a good student and the rabbi had chosen me to go on to the yeshiva in Odessa to study!"

"I too am something of a student," I reply. "I study already at the yeshiva in Odessa. I'll tell you what," I suggest. "Every Sunday when we go to church we will each develop a talk, as if we are the rabbi speaking to our congregation. After church we will tell each other what we have developed and you will criticize mine, and I will criticize yours. And as we march we will discuss Torah together. They have baptized us by force but we can still work on our Jewishness."

"What about the food?" he whispers. "I've only eaten bread and tea."

"You must eat the pork," I command. "You must live and return to your family. We'll do it together."

He looks at me then, grateful for a friend, grateful not to be alone. Our eyes meet. We have made a bond.

After that, when all are converted or dead, we begin to march. On the first day of the march a boy comes up to us and interrupts Samuel and me while we argue a point of Torah. He is very tall, with broad shoulders and a thatch of red hair. His face is covered in freckles. He grins at us. I recognize him immediately. He was the first to be baptized, as soon as they demanded it, and gobbled the pork down with relish.

"This conversation is pointless," he booms at us.

"What!" Samuel declares, obviously furious.

"Pointless," he repeats. "Why not discuss something of value, like the state of the peasants and how a whole new order is needed. Who cares about the legal implications of this law or that! Worry about how the rich have everything, the poor nothing, and what we can do to change that!"

Samuel looks as if he is about to hit him, which would be silly since Samuel is about half this boy's size.

"Well," I say, trying to make peace, "I think that would be very interesting to talk about. *After* we finish this discussion."

"My name is Josef." The boy grins, "and I'll be glad to wait."

And he does. He waits until Samuel and I finish our discussion and then tells us all about himself.

"I'm an atheist," he announces, "so I don't care what they call me. I attended one of the new schools set up by the czar before I was conscripted. Our village is small and all the boys from age fifteen are in the army now. Next year they will take the fourteen-year-olds." He shakes his head. "The whole system must be swept away!" he declares.

I have to smile. His enthusiasm is infectious, and although he is the complete opposite of Samuel, I know I will like him equally as much. It occurs to me that it is dangerous to make friends when life is so uncertain. I realize it would be safer to remain completely alone. Many choose that path rather than risk the heartbreak of losing someone close to you. But how can one live without friendship, without love?

It is the friendship of these two boys that sustains me over the next few weeks, for we march endlessly. All day we march; at night we sleep in the open, only rarely reaching a town where we can shelter in the barracks. Winter has come early and soon it will be Hanukah, although I've lost track of the exact time of month, and the weather is unusually cold.

Somewhere Sukkos came and went, as did Simkhas Torah, both holidays always celebrated with such joy in our home. I remember being so proud when I was a young boy because my mother made me the best Sukkos banner in our neighborhood; she always made an ark with doors that actually opened and drew two huge lions to guard it. I would march around in shul with the other boys, holding my banner high. And I remember after my Bar Mitzvah at age thirteen, when I was allowed to carry a real Torah and how terrified I was that I would drop it and bring calamity down on the entire congregation. It almost seems as if these things happened to another boy in another life. From the twelve boys we began with in Odessa, only four have survived. So far. The rest gave up. One by one they lay down along the road, fever burning through their eyes, and did not get up again. One hung himself the last time we were in a barracks. Another stabbed himself with a knife.

Finally we arrive at a barracks and are allowed to sleep with a roof over our heads. All the recruits are asleep but I am so overtired I can't rest. I get out of my bunk and pad to the door. There is a light on in a room down the hall, and I can hear voices raised in anger. I creep out into the hallway and listen. It is Sergei, the sergeant, and the blond private whose name, I have finally discovered, is Lopov. I've never heard him referred to by a first name, only Lopov. Lopov is yelling. He sounds drunk.

"It's all very well for you, Sergei. You make good money out of this. But what about me? I march day in, day out, for the few extra kopecks you give me."

"I give you plenty," Sergei replies, his words slurred.

"Not enough!" Lopov yells. "We are given much money to transport the brats to Siberia by wagon and I want some of it. And what about the money we save on food?"

"All right, all right, Lopov, calm down," I hear Sergei say. "I can spare you a bit more. But," he adds, his voice threatening, "don't ever forget who's in charge here. Oh, yes, I could make your life miserable."

"How?" comes Lopov's voice. "How could it be more miserable. Marching to Siberia with a bunch of disgusting Yids. This is no work for a soldier. The only pleasure I get is when they drop off like flies, or better yet, do themselves in."

Then I hear a chair scraping so I hurry back to my cot and pretend to sleep. But I can't sleep. I keep going over it in my head, again and again. So they'd been given money to transport us but they are pocketing it, and that is why we are marching. And the food—that's why our rations have dropped so drastically. Often all we eat all day is dry biscuits. It is cold-blooded murder for money, nothing less. All those boys who fell by the road, chilled through by the wind and the snow, weak from lack of food. . . . I haven't cried since I've been captured. But tonight I put my head down into the thin mattress and I weep. I weep for those that have died, weep for the heartless cruelty I have discovered in people, I weep for myself. I do not know who I am anymore; I don't know what I have become. Life doesn't seem worth living when such horrors can happen. Perhaps I should give up, end it all. Suddenly revenge and hate and even love are no longer enough to sustain me. But then an idea comes to me out of nowhere. In the middle of all that black despair, this little idea enters my brain. If the sergeant has money, then there is money to steal. And if I can steal it, I can use it to escape. But where? Where can I go? Dressed in army garb perhaps I could sneak across the border into Romania. And if I could do that, perhaps I could get away from Russia altogether. I'd go to England, I'd send for Miriam, and I'd never set foot in this country again. Perhaps God, if He exists, has sent me this idea. Perhaps my guardian angel. Whatever, it gets me through the night.

Now I try to ingratiate myself even more with the sergeant. I march near him, sleep near him, help him as a translator. I watch him constantly. I am sure I know where the money is. He has a small leather pouch that is tied with cord to his belt. He pats it before he beds down at night, and in the morning when he wakes up it is the first thing he checks. I can't imagine how I am going to get it away from him. Then I realize that I will need help. And I know whom I will ask. I will confide in Samuel and Josef. And perhaps together we will plan our escape.

ZED

This can't be happening to me. It's some sort of huge, stupid mistake.

"This is a mistake!" I scream, but the soldiers continue to pull me down the street. The captain swats me on the back of the head.

"No Yiddish!" he screams. He speaks in Russian. I can understand it better than I can speak it. He's telling me to speak Russian or not to bother speaking at all.

I try to explain in my broken Russian that I can get him three or four boys, that I am a khapper, but he laughs.

"We like *you!*" he roars, and smacks me again across the ears so hard they start to ring.

I am pulled into an old building that the army must be using for their recruits. There are about a dozen young boys already there, some very young, perhaps eight or ten years old. They are swamped in huge army coats and their heads are shaved. They wear boots obviously many sizes too big. They look at me, their expressions blank, as if they feel nothing. I am dragged into an empty room. A soldier throws clothes on the floor and gestures for me to undress. I shake my head. I can't let them do this to me! He punches me, hard, in the stomach. I double over, coughing. He kicks me in the ribs, then the backside, sending me sprawling. The others laugh and talk in Russian. I think they are telling this new soldier that I am a khapper. He seems to find this funny. He laughs and gives me another kick. I can't stand the pain. I gesture for him to stop. I draw the clothes to me and change, carefully slipping my money bag into my new coat. I cling to the hope that I can use it to buy my way out of here.

Someone pushes me into a chair. My head is shaved. Then they motion me out into the larger room where the other boys wait. They've managed to find me a pair of boots that is too small. I show the guards, pointing, pleading, trying to get them to change the boots. They ignore me. I want to be allowed my own boots but they just give me another smack, then send us all out the door.

We are put in a wagon, driven to a synagogue. It is filled with people. Russian officials, the kahal, including Mr. Meyer, and some rabbis. We are led to the Bimah and made to recite an oath to the czar.

When we are finished they blow the shofar and with each blast of the ram's horn I know that I am lost forever. If I try to desert now, they have the right to kill me. I realize that I am theirs.

We are herded out of the synagogue and into a wagon. We sit there together, squashed against one another, as the wagon bumps along the road. We aren't given lunch, and when we have to relieve ourselves we are forced to jump from the wagon, do our business, then run after it. A soldier throws me back in so hard I knock over a number of boys. As evening falls we get out at a barracks in another town to join up with a larger group. We are pushed into a hall full of Cantonist reservists—in other words, Jewish children. There are perhaps a hundred seated at long tables. The battalion commander stands at the front of the room waiting for us to be seated, then he starts to scream in Russian. I can only understand bits of it, but he has a young boy translate. When the boy speaks too quietly he hits the boy across the back with a thick wooden rod.

"I want you all to know," the boy yells, his voice high and squeaky, "that there will not be one Jew left in this regiment by the time I am finished, so get yourselves baptized or I will flog each and every one of you to death!"

A shiver of fear and horror runs through me and yet at the same time I feel like laughing because the words sound so silly coming out of this little boy. About a dozen priests step forward from behind the commander.

He roars an order. The boy translates. "Those of you who want to take the step now, come forward. The rest—be warned."

About twenty go forward and leave the room with the priests. Cowards. Don't they know they'll pay for their fear? God will not forgive them. Too easily they forget about the world to come, life after this one, but not me. I never forget such things.

"Take off your coats," he orders. "And your shirts." He shows us with gestures, pushing the young boy away.

Slowly they all do. I do it quickly, throwing my shirt on the floor, showing them I am not afraid. One soldier takes each row. They pull long rods out of huge vats of water. I have to sit at the table and wait patiently while they flog those beside me. I have to listen to their screams. I will not scream.

Shall I fight? Perhaps it would be better to die fighting. I will never convert. Never. They can kill me first. Oh, yes, it is one thing to kidnap for them and get paid for it. After all, someone had to do it. If it hadn't been me, it would have been someone else. And I needed the money. I could have helped my family. God understands that. In fact I believe He approves. But He would never understand conversion. Never.

I think of the money in my coat. I have to be patient. If I can get one of these louts alone I can probably buy my way out of here. I just have to get through this first.

Whack! The rod hits my back with such force that

I let out an involuntary scream and fall forward, hitting my head on the table. I didn't even see him coming. Whack! I can feel it cutting through my skin, and now I know why the rods were soaking in water. It's salt water. The cut burns like fire. Whack! I close my eyes and bite on my lip so hard I can feel warm blood flowing. How long will this last? The room is filled with screams and moans.

The rod stops. I am a mass of pain. The commander is yelling. Now the little reedy voice of the translator cuts through the screams. "He wants everyone to go outside, but don't put your clothes back on."

We are lined up outdoors. It is terribly cold. Unusually cold. A north wind blows. I stare at the back of the boy in front of me. Is that what I look like? Long red streaks cover his back, oozing blood. I hear a terrible scream and try to see where it's coming from. Soldiers carrying buckets of water are moving down the line. They are pouring water over the heads and backs of the recruits. I grit my teeth and await my turn. When it comes it is almost unbearable. I see many have fainted and I gasp as the icy water hits my wounds. My head spins and I feel like keeling over but I won't allow myself to. No, I vow, they will not shake me. I will live on my terms or not at all.

We are forced to stand in the snow, the wind blowing on us, until one by one the recruits give in and are led away to the priests. Around ten lie in the snow, dead or dying. I stand alone. It is dark now and the soldiers are tired. Finally they motion me indoors. I return to the large room where the newly converted are now dressed and are eating hot borscht, tea, and bread. I notice that some, despite their newfound religion, eat only the tea and bread. Fools. Do they think God will be tricked by that? I am allowed to put on my clothes, but I am given no food, nothing to drink. I almost pass out from pain, hunger, fatigue. But I will not. Finally, we are shown into huge dormitories, with only straw on the floor. We all lie down, on our stomachs. Even though I am exhausted I can't say I really sleep. I slip in and out of consciousness, and I dream. Sometimes I see Aaron. That is my only consolation. Whatever I am going through, it is comforting to know that he has gone through it too. But he is not as strong as I am. Perhaps he chose to die. Good. I hope so. If it wasn't for him and his family I wouldn't be here. They chased me out of town so fast that I forgot my papers. It is all *their* fault. My hatred for him grows and grows. I hope he suffered. I hope he suffers still.

Finally morning comes. Everyone is given food but me. Then we are forced outside to begin our march. We are headed for Siberia where we will be trained. A new pain is now added to the one in my back. My boots squeeze my toes and every step becomes agony. I can feel blisters and sores forming and I begin to limp. Finally I cannot go on. The soldier nearby looks at me.

"Convert," he says, "and you can have a new pair of boots. Ones that fit."

I remove my boots, and leaving them in the road, I walk. At first the cold snow on my feet is a relief to the sores and blisters, but soon I realize that my feet are beginning to freeze and they will not move. I decide that I must put my money to good use now, or die.

I call the soldier back. In my best Russian I try to explain to him that I have money, lots of it, and that I will give it all to him if he helps me escape. He demands to see it. I pull the bag out, keeping my coat around it so no one else can see, and show him the contents. He smiles and nods. I knew it! I knew I would succeed.

"You wait," he says to me with a wink, and he goes forward to the supply wagon. He returns with a good pair of boots and motions me to drop out of the line. I do so. I try on the boots. They fit—not perfectly, but well enough. Then he takes a thick piece of black bread from his pocket and puts it in mine along with a stack of dry biscuits. I smile. He smiles back. Most of his teeth are rotted through; it's disgusting. Then he punches me hard in the stomach. I double over and he hits me on the head. I fall face first into the snow. He bends over and whispers in my ear as he reaches under me and grabs my money, "I'll get you food, Yid, for the money. But escape, never! Now get up and march!"

I stagger to my feet and he pushes me back into

the marching line. Pain shoots through the back of my head where he hit me. That's it then, my last hope gone. Still, I can see God is with me. He doesn't want me to convert, and as long as I am given food I will hold out and live. If He wants me to die, I will do that too.

I will always be a good Jew. These weaklings around me deserve what they will get when they die and meet their Maker.

CHAPTER 9

Aaron

Samuel, Josef, and I sit in a small circle, our teeth chattering, trying to shelter ourselves from the wind. The soldiers and sergeants sleep by their horses or the wagons for warmth, and keep fires going. We are forced to lie in our greatcoats all night and we must hope we won't die of cold before morning. Tomorrow night we will sleep in a barracks in another town.

I feel it will be our best chance, perhaps last chance to escape. We are to meet another group of recruits there, and travel with them to Siberia.

Samuel does not look well. I am worried about him. His eyes have the bright cast of fever. He has tried. He has eaten the soup with hunks of pork and fat floating in it but then he throws it all up. All he can keep down is tea, bread, and sometimes the borscht, which doesn't taste as strongly of pig. He is very thin, and often when we do our Torah studies he forgets, as if his brain will no longer work under these conditions. Josef, on the other hand, seems to take it all in stride, his good humor never flagging.

"I want to escape," I tell them both.

Josef laughs, his laugh a roar big as a bear's. I see the fear in Samuel's eyes.

"I'm serious," I protest. "Sergei has money. Lots of money. He's pocketed our transportation fees. That's why we're marching to Siberia. Also he's cheating on the food supplies."

Samuel shakes his head. "All those who have died," he whispers, "he may as well have slit their throats."

"Exactly," I agree. "And we don't want to be next," I add pointedly. Josef and I exchange a look. He too realizes that Samuel is getting weaker and weaker by the day. "We have to steal the money. Then we'll steal horses and use the money to bribe our way to safety. We'll travel to Romania and from there, somehow, we'll get to England."

Again Josef laughs.

"Quiet," I say, "do you want everyone to notice us?"

"It's a fairy tale," Josef chuckles. "A lovely one, but a fairy tale nevertheless. First, how do we steal the money? Second, how do we get to Romania? Third, how do we get to England without papers?"

"Number one," I say, refusing to be discouraged,

"whenever we stay in a barracks our friend Sergei gets drunk and passes out. It only takes some courage to sneak into his room and steal the money. We slip away while everyone is drunk and asleep. We steal three horses and ride. Number two, if we are stopped and asked for our papers, we use the money for bribes to get across the frontier. Number three, we bribe our way to England."

"And if we fail," Samuel says, "we'll be beaten or forced to run the gauntlet."

"For you, Samuel," I say gently, "there is little choice. This is your only hope. But Josef, you should consider. You will survive this life and one day return home."

"And you?" Josef asks. "You too will survive."

"No," I answer, "I won't. I have lived this long because I have never given up the hope that I can escape. Without that, I would have given up long ago. I must try. And if I die, so be it, perhaps it is God's will."

Josef snorts. He doesn't think anything is God's will. And as for me, I'm not sure anymore what God wants of me. It used to be so clear. Keep the commandments. Follow the laws. Eat kosher. Pray. And now that I am deprived of all that, now that I wear a cross around my neck, what does God want of me? What?

"I will think about it," Josef says.

Then we all huddle together for warmth and try to sleep.

We march all the next day and not until twilight

do we finally reach the town. The barracks are the same as all the others. We move into a large room filled with rows of tables. We line up for our hot borscht and black bread. There is already another regiment in the room, just finishing their food. They get up to go to the sleeping quarters and file past us. Samuel, Josef, and I wait in line together.

Something catches my eye. A memory. A face. A look. I stare. Someone is coming toward me. At first I can't understand. It looks exactly like Zev Lobonsky. But of course that isn't possible. He would be the last person to be here, in a Cantonist battalion. Him, a khapper. But it looks so much like him. The face is thinner, the shoulders slightly stooped, but. . . . He straightens his shoulders and then his glance settles on me. He stops. Those behind him start to push, not wanting to get beaten for causing trouble by moving too slowly. They shove him close to me, closer. I have pictured this moment so often, dreamed it, imagined it, how I would put my hands around his throat and not let go until all the breath had left him. But what do I do? I stand. I stare. I am frozen. I cannot move. He too seems unable to move or speak. He is pushed by those behind him until he is right beside me and I gaze into his eyes and the black soul behind them. Before I know what I am doing I spit at him full in the face. I see his look of shock, hate, disgust, and then he is pushed on and he is out the door. Samuel and Josef drag me over to a table and force me onto a bench. I am trembling from head to foot.

"What is it?" Samuel asks. "Who was it? Not—?"

I had told them the story of my capture and had often whispered my plans of revenge as we walked or just before we slept.

I nod, still unable to speak.

"But how?" Josef wonders aloud. "He was a khapper."

I know they are talking but I cannot really pay attention to them. My mind is whirling. He is here. The maker of all my misery is here. I have vowed to kill him. I must kill him. I must seek him out, as he sleeps, and I must show him no mercy. I want to hear him weep, beg my forgiveness, I want to see him die.

Josef is shaking me. He puts a spoon in my hand.

"Eat," he commands. "You are weak from the march today. You must eat."

I obey him. I put the spoon to my mouth, I swallow. I eat my bread. Their voices come to me as if from far away.

"Aaron, Aaron, wake up!" Samuel admonishes me. "Come back to the real world."

Slowly I look at him and try to concentrate on what he says.

"Aaron, he's here. All your dreams of revenge are within your grasp. Aaron, listen to me." He shakes me hard by the shoulders. "If you do it, you're no better than him. Is that what you want?"

"Never mind about that!" Josef says. "Moral decisions are one thing, practical decisions are another. If you kill him, the army will kill you. And what about us? What about our plans for escape? We need you in order to do it. Only your Russian is good enough to fool the people on the way. Aaron," he says, almost into my ear, "without you, Samuel won't make it. What's more important? Him or your revenge?"

I stare at them both. I am filled with such hate, such bitterness, it is pouring through me, I can feel, but I can't think. My brain, my thoughts, seem to have stopped, frozen like ice on a pond in winter.

"It has to be tonight," Josef whispers in my ear. "Zev can only make trouble for you now. Tonight or never."

We are getting up from our tables, going to the big room where we will sleep. Heaps of straw litter the floor. Still I am thankful to be indoors. Samuel and Josef lie down, one on either side of me. Soon the room is filled with deep breathing, the constant coughing of some of the boys sick and weak from the march, the quiet moaning of others as they sleep and pray for death to release them.

I try to calm myself. I have been trained since I was a child to think clearly, to look at all sides of a problem. To be logical. And yet, it seems that I have become nothing more than wild, confused emotions—and my feelings do me no credit. They are base and low—what is worse than anger and hate? But not only do I hate Zev, I hate myself too. After all, look what I have become. I have broken God's most serious prohibition—I have converted. And besides, I can feel no pity or empathy for Zev, only the desire to have my revenge. Perhaps I should kill him and then take the consequences. I deserve no better.

I think of Miriam. I remember her smile. I can see her eyes flash as we argue a point. And suddenly before me her eyes flash and she glares at me and demands, "And me, Aaron, what about me? Won't you even try to escape, to return to me? Doesn't God also want us to marry, have children, lead good lives?"

"But Miriam," I reply, "you wouldn't want me anyway. Not when you understand what kind of person I really am."

"You let me decide that!" she declares.

I have to smile. Here I am, having an imaginary conversation with my bride-to-be. Perhaps I *have* lost my mind.

But when I think of Miriam I get such a rush of love it almost overpowers me. At least I can still feel love, as well as hate. And if I can feel love perhaps I am not completely worthless. And what of Josef and Samuel? I have come to love them too. They are like brothers. Can I disappoint them? They will never succeed without me. In fact, if I go after Zev now, and die because of it, Zev will have succeeded in what he set out to do. And then there is the teaching: an eye for an eye. Zev must be suffering as I am. According to law I cannot ask for more—I cannot ask for his death. And I will not give him his final triumph—my death. I will deny him that.

"We go tonight," I say to my friends. "Zev is not worth dying for."

Josef hits me on the back.

"Good for you!" he whispers. "And," he adds, "I'm with you, Aaron. We will all go together."

We lie awake, staring into the darkness. My heart pounds so loudly I am sure it will wake those sleeping near me. Soon we hear the familiar sounds of Sergei and Lopov fighting and swearing at each other, both drunk out of their wits.

"Not long now," I whisper to Samuel and Josef. "In moments they'll be out cold in a drunken stupor."

It seems like forever, though, until their voices die down and finally all is silent. My heart in my throat, I rise and motion for the others to follow. We pad across the room. The passageway is dark but a dim light flickers from the adjacent room. We reach the doorway. We see both men slumped in their chairs, a candle sputtering on the table. The smell of cheap vodka is overwhelming. We creep into the room. Lopov is reclining in his chair but Sergei has fallen forward, his head on the table. We will have to move him to get the money bag.

Slowly, ever so slowly, Samuel and Josef shift him so that his back leans against his chair. He snorts and almost wakens but is too drunk to pull himself out of his stupor. I kneel beside him and gingerly begin to fiddle with the string which attaches the bag to his belt. It is knotted well but I work quickly. I have to put all my effort into stilling the shaking of my hands. Finally it is loose. I open it, peer inside. It is filled with kopecks. More than enough for my plan. I nod to the others, tuck it into the pocket of my coat, and we creep toward the door.

Suddenly a shadow falls across the doorway. There blocking our exit is Zev. Zev Lobonsky.

"I've been looking for you!" he whispers.

CHAPTER 10

ZEV

I stand in the doorway, blocking their way, grinning from ear to ear.

"What are you up to then?" I say.

I don't think I'll kill Aaron, that would only get me shot. No. I'll get him in so much trouble he'll wish he were dead. Perhaps, just being here, in this room, is enough for the soldiers to shoot Aaron and his friends. I hope so. It is his fault I'm here. Him and his stupid father. He has made me suffer. Now I'll have my revenge.

One of the boys with Aaron is big. He takes a step toward me.

"One more move and I'll wake up the entire regiment," I say. "Won't they be interested in finding you all here?"

Aaron is glaring at me with so much hate in his eyes I almost laugh.

"And what is going on inside of your brainy head?" I ask him, my tone mocking. "You have no reason to hate me. I was only doing my job!"

He stares at me for another full minute, then his look changes from one of pure hate to disgust mixed with disbelief.

"You can't mean that!" he says, the first words he has managed to speak to me. "You can't honestly believe that?" His voice drops now. It is low and intense. "You put me here. You kidnapped me in the forest, you dragged me away from my family, my friends, from . . . everyone I loved."

Oh, I know whom he's thinking about.

"You mean the lovely Miriam," I answer with a snicker. "She and I had a little talk in her barn just before I left. She liked me. A lot. It was only a matter of time before I won her over."

His friends are holding on to him, one on each arm, to stop him from going for me.

"That is, until *your* family got me into this mess. They came after me, a crazy mob. I had to run, left my papers behind—and, well, a Jew without papers is as good as in the army, isn't he? So you see, little scholar, it's all your fault that I am here. You and your cursed family."

Aaron looks at me as if he can't believe his ears. I suppose he can't understand that he or his family could ever do anything wrong.

"You're mad," he answers. "Mad," he repeats. "This is all *your* doing, not mine. At least be a man and admit it. Admit it!"

"I admit nothing," I say. "No, it is your fault I am here. You have dogged me all my life. You are the student my father wanted me to be, the young man Miriam wanted instead of me, and now because of you, I'm here, in this place, a place not even fit for animals."

I step into the room so that I'm not seen should anyone wander down the corridor. It's unlikely though since I waited until everyone was asleep and all the soldiers and commanders had drunk themselves into unconsciousness.

"So what are you three up to then?" I ask again.

This is really very interesting. What are they doing here in a room with these two soldiers? What is going on? Is it something I can use to really make their lives miserable? I have the power to hurt them now and it feels wonderful.

"Tell me," I command, "or I'll wake the whole place up!"

"Now, now, don't be hasty." The big fellow takes another step forward. "We'll tell you."

Aaron looks at him in alarm.

"No, we won't!" he says.

"We heard fighting," the big fellow says. "Aaron and this sergeant have become friendly, in a way. Aaron was worried that he would be hurt. We came to check, make sure everything was all right."

Could this be true? It sounds just like something Aaron would do. He'd rush to help some Russian who'd probably just as soon see him dead. He makes me sick.

"And what's going on here may I ask?"

I whirl around. It's the commander of my battalion! He's weaving sideways and trying to see clearly through his drunken fog. Weeks ago when he finally realized that I would never convert, and that somehow I managed to survive (he didn't know I was secretly getting food), he told me I would be his helper, getting new recruits to convert. I didn't mind. He gives me special treatment, and if I didn't do it one of his soldiers would. Besides, those Jewish recruits deserve what they get—they are so weak they make me sick.

"Well, well, well, if it isn't my little helper." He slaps me on the back. He looks at the three boys who are staring at him, terror written all over their faces.

"Are you going to make them kneel all night until they convert?" he asks me. "We did a good job on that last bunch, didn't we?" He looks closer. My head is thudding. What do I tell him? He's so drunk maybe he'll just wander off. "So, Yid, what are you doing here? I asked you a question."

"I heard voices," I answer. "So I came to make sure it wasn't any of our lads. I found these three here. I don't know what they were up to." I pause. I think. This is it. My chance! My revenge!

"But after investigating, I am quite sure they planned to rob these poor soldiers who are lying here unable to defend themselves."

"Yes," he roars, "that must be it. Stinking rotten lousy Jews! Money's all they care about. Rob us."

He turns his glare on me and whaps me across the face with the back of his hand so hard that I fall to my knees. "You too. You make me sick. You're probably in on it with them! I'll have you all shot!"

His voice is getting louder and louder. Soon the whole barracks will wake up. The blond soldier begins to stir.

"No, no," I plead, still on my knees, "you can't believe that. I'm your helper. Aren't I the one who stood over those boys day and night for you, never letting them sleep, or eat? You can't think I'm like them!"

He kicks me in the stomach with the toe of his boot. I double over, retching.

"You're a stinking Yid," he sneers, "and you make me sick."

And then, so fast that I only see it from the corner of my eye, the big one moves. He punches the commander so hard across the jaw that the commander staggers back, hits his head against the wall, and falls to the ground. I look up. He's unconscious. "Let's get out of here," the big fellow says.

I stagger to my feet.

"I'm going with you," I whisper, trying to catch my breath. "If I stay he'll have me shot." I glare at Aaron. "You again. Because of you. Now I have no choice."

Aaron stares at me. "You can't come. We're deserting. And we don't want you along."

"I'm a dead man if I stay," I reply. "Either you take me with you, or I scream my head off, wake up the whole place. I've nothing to lose. And don't try knocking me out," I say, warning the big guy. "I'll put up a big fight and we'll never get out of here."

Aaron puts his hand on the big one's arm. "No time," he says. "We must leave now. He'll have to come." I hear him mutter to himself. "I'll deal with him later."

"Or I'll deal with you," I snarl. "Let's go."

We creep down the hall. It's dark and quiet. We reach the outer door and slip outside. We see a guard's back as he rounds the side of the building. That was close.

And so I follow him and his friends into the cold and the dark. And I vow that if and when I am safe, I will kill him, the cause of all my misery.

CHAPTER 11

Aaron

I'm escaping, and with me is the person who got me here in the first place. It's completely mad. It will put an unbearable strain on our escape, for he will have to be watched constantly, he can never be trusted. My head is still whirling from the words which spewed from his mouth. He really seems to believe that his misfortunes are all my fault and that he is not to blame for anything. It is terrifying to realize that he feels no remorse and will not even admit he has done anything wrong! I force myself to try to get these thoughts out of my mind—I must concentrate on only one thing now, our escape.

We creep across the dark yard toward the stables. Only Josef knows anything about horses; he will have to show us how to saddle them. Riding is, I hope, just a matter of holding on very tightly. Normally the stables are guarded but all the guards are off somewhere, probably dead drunk. We slip through the stable door. It's pitch black. The horses sense our presence and begin to whinny nervously.

"We must be quick," Josef says, "or they'll make such a racket someone is bound to find us."

Zev's voice grates through the darkness. "The blankets and saddles will be slung over the railing by each stall. Who else can put them on?"

"I can," Josef replies.

"Well, let Aaron help you, and the other one can help me. Hurry up!"

I have no choice but to listen. Josef and I feel our way over to a stall. He pats the animal and mumbles soothing words. I feel for the blanket and gently put it over the horse's back. Josef slings the saddle on. The reins and the bit are harder to find. Finally we get our hands on them but they are very difficult to manage in the dark. I am becoming more panic-stricken by the moment. What a crazy idea this was! Even if we escape from these barracks, how will I ever ride one of these animals? They are so huge, so terrifying. Every time the horse snorts or stamps its foot, my heart lands in my throat.

And then what? We ride, if we can, through the snows to the frontier? Certainly they will follow us. They will have to find us or they themselves will be punished.

"All right, Aaron, I'm done. We'll go to the next stall now," Josef whispers, interrupting my thoughts.

I follow him, dutifully, feeling sick about what I've gotten us all into.

"Perhaps you should return to the barracks," I whisper to him as we work. "You could tell them it was all my fault. They'd probably give you a beating and leave it at that."

Josef snorts, sounding for a moment just like one of the horses.

"They'll beat us to death," he answers. "And you know it."

After what seems like years the horses are ready. I tiptoe to the stable door and peek out. All is quiet. We take the horses by the reins and slowly lead them out. The one I have stamps his feet and holds back. It could be that I've chosen an officer's horse and he will not willingly go with anyone else. Wonderful. Gently I pull him forward, trying to think of encouraging words to say.

"Come, you stupid animal," I mutter, keeping my voice soothing, "try to show more intelligence than your cousin the mule. That's it. Good beast. Never fear. You can easily kill me when I'm in the saddle."

The moon is out, three-quarters full, and the sky is clear, bright with stars. Our breath and the breath of the horses fog the air. A light dusting of snow sparkles around us like millions of tiny diamonds. There is no wind. The silence is terrifying. Suddenly my horse neighs wildly.

"Mount." Josef's whisper is urgent. "We must

ride." He helps me into the saddle, then Samuel. Zev is already mounted, waiting impatiently.

"Who goes there?"

The voice comes from the side of the barracks, cutting through the night air like a sword.

Josef leaps onto his horse and kicks it into motion. I do the same. The heaving bulk beneath me that had been shifting nervously seems to leap in the air, then, with a shrill whinny, it takes off after Josef. I have to stop myself from screaming in fear. Samuel follows me; Zev brings up the rear. We gallop out to the main road. I hang on desperately to the reins and the saddle and begin saying the Shema, sure that these will be my last moments on earth. Then I remember I had said these words, for the last time, the night I converted. Never mind, who cares, I think, and say them again. *Sh'ma yisroayl, Adonoy elohaynu, Adonoy ehod.* The prayer one says before one dies. Why did I do this? I would have survived the army. I could have lived. This was a stupid idea and now there's no going back. Did that guard see anything? Are they coming after us already? I don't dare turn around to look, afraid that if I twist my body even a little, I will lose my balance completely and fall off. My body is pounding into the horse, which is not galloping but trotting very fast, so that my teeth seem to rattle in my mouth and I keep hitting the saddle with all my weight.

I know that we are headed in the direction of the Romanian frontier and that it will probably take us at least two days to reach it. I can see the map I used to study at school in my mind's eye. I have a plan. I hope it will work. We will find out in the morning if we manage to make it to the next town without being caught. This is not the road the troops will be taking. They will veer off north and head for Siberia. I sink low over the saddle and press my legs into the horse's body in an effort to hang on tighter. We dare not slow the pace, so Josef keeps the lead and we follow. I am grateful that at least my horse follows his.

The night passes in this way. As morning comes I can feel a warmer breeze stirring and clouds moving in. Josef slows his horse and we all gather in the road, which is solid because of the unusual cold. I dread to think what it would have been like had we been slogging through mud. I try not to look at Zev. Just the sight of him makes me feel ill.

"What now?" Josef asks as our horses stand, panting and exhausted beneath us.

"We enter the next town," I say, "before daybreak. I happen to know there is a Jewish section. We go straight there."

"They'll hide us?" Samuel says hopefully.

"No, no," I reply, "we won't let on we're Jews. How do we know whom we can trust? What we do know is that they are terrified of Russian soldiers. Whatever we ask for we'll be given, no questions asked. We'll get food. My plan is to find someone who can help us cross the border."

"Why not just go ourselves?" Zev chides. "That way we don't need to trust anyone. We simply find out where the border crossing is, get a look at the land, and cross over somewhere. They can't watch it all. We can go right into Romania. Easy."

I glare at him, about to tell him to shut up.

"He's right," Josef says to me. "It *is* better to trust no one. Let's get some food and then lie low for the day. How far are we from the border?"

"At least another day's ride," I answer. "But we don't dare travel during the day."

"There may not be a moon tonight," Josef counters. "I think we should get food and be on our way. We'll move off the main road and travel across the fields."

"But it's completely open," Zev objects. "Anyone could see us. And they'd wonder why we aren't on the road."

"Even without a moon, the snow's reflection gives enough light," I suggest. "I think we should travel at night." I turn to Zev. "You can leave anytime. You have a horse. You can sneak across the border on your own. No need to stay here with us."

He stares at me. "No," he answers slowly, "I'm not ready to leave yet."

I open my mouth to reply when Samuel speaks.

"Perhaps he'd better stay with us, Aaron. After all, once he leaves we can't be certain that he won't turn us in."

Zev makes that grating noise which I suppose he would call a laugh. "Your little friend is so right," he says. "Now let's move along here. It's getting light fast."

Reluctantly I agree to let him stay and we hasten toward the town. There is a tavern right on the outskirts as we approach. Josef and Zev dismount. I try but find it isn't all that easy. My leg muscles seem to have cramped up in such a way that as I try to straighten them they scream in protest. My horse starts to stamp impatiently. Josef comes up, holds him by the bit, and speaks to him in an effort to calm him down.

"Swing your leg over and get down," he orders.

I try but my leg gets caught in my long coat and suddenly I am hanging headfirst, my left foot stuck in the stirrup.

Zev seems to find this hilarious and starts making that annoying grating sound again. I spot Josef trying not to laugh as well, although it's hard to tell people's expressions when you're hanging upside down. Josef comes to my rescue. He gets my foot untangled with one hand and breaks my fall with his other arm. Samuel had managed to dismount without incident. Josef and Samuel look at each other and I can see they are dying to laugh, but since Zev is doing enough of that they restrain themselves.

We stare at the tavern.

"I'll go," I say to Josef. "My Russian is best."

"Remember," Josef whispers to me, "if they are Jewish, offer nothing. A Russian doesn't have to explain anything to a Jew. They'll be so afraid of us they'll never think to ask what we're doing here. If they are peasants you must be ready to bribe them."

I walk around the side of the tavern. I knock. A

middle-aged man opens the tavern door. I can see right away he is Jewish. He wears a talis koton and a yarmulke. "We want food, shelter, and care for our horses," I demand.

For a moment he looks at me, unsure, then turns to a younger man who stands behind a counter. The younger man nods.

"Come in, then," he says.

I go to fetch the others. They follow me into the tavern. The smell of food assaults us and almost makes me faint. In fact I sway and have to catch at a table for support. I ease myself into a chair. The others join me. It is a small tavern, plain, humble but not poor. The wood floors are clean, there are many tables, and because of the barn for cows in the back, it reminds me of Miriam's family's tavern. A woman in her forties, her gray hair struggling out of her scarf, her face lined, comes out of the back room. She carries a tray full of fresh bread, butter and cheese, and herring. She places it on our table. For a moment we all just stare at it. I see her shuffle nervously, perhaps afraid it is not to our liking. I rip off a piece of bread, put a herring on it, and take my first bite. I could die now and be happy. My first kosher meal since joining the army. The taste is indescribable.

She sees the expression on my face, nods, and hurries away. She returns with tea. The tray is empty and I ask her for more. She gets more. We eat until we can eat no more. I look at Samuel. He has eaten his first real meal in months. He grins at me. I whisper to the others.

"I told him we'd want to sleep near our horses. They are feeding them and putting them in their barn. The cows have been milked. We can sleep in the straw there. I told him we'd want dinner there after dark and that we'd pay him well. I said we were on a secret mission and that if he said anything about us to anyone, he'd regret it."

"Time to go to the barn then," Josef says. "Too many eyes will be here soon."

We push back our chairs and head out to the barn. The horses have been well tended to. We each find a pile of straw and throw ourselves on it. I hope we're doing the right thing. I hope the garrison won't catch up with us today, and if they do, I hope this innkeeper is too scared to give us away. Does he suspect, I wonder? Can he tell from our looks that we're Jewish? Or too young to be soldiers? He must know he'd be in terrible trouble for hiding us. But he also knows that if we *are* Russian, he could get in more trouble for not hiding us. I hope he'll reason that he has little choice but to help. I just hope we don't bring ruin down on him and his family. I just hope we can make it through this day.

I look at Zev. He is lying on the straw, relaxed, no doubt plotting against me. Why have we been thrown together like this? Do I dare sleep? Will he try to kill me? Or, my hate for him as strong as ever, will I try to kill him?

ZEV

I can't rest. I lie here, on the bed of straw, and
wonder at the events that have brought Aaron and
me together like this. Maybe it's a message from
God. Am I being punished for being a khapper? Is
that why I'm here? But I can't believe that God
would be angry at me for that. I watch as Aaron
takes off his coat and then I see it—the cross. So
he has converted! The scholar, the revered jewel of
Odessa, has converted! Now I know why God has
thrown us together. I am His servant and He wants
Aaron punished. I will be God's right hand. I will
make Aaron sorry he was so weak, his Judaism
meant so little to him. I'll punish him for God and
I'll have my revenge on him. If it wasn't for Aaron
I would still be in Odessa, ready to buy my own
house. I would be rich, prosperous, feared. Instead,

I've been living like an animal, groveling to my commander, fighting every day just to stay alive. That meal, that herring and fresh bread, reminded me so much of everything I miss. No, Aaron will pay, and soon. I'll do it tonight or tomorrow as we try to cross the border. That's when it will be the easiest to get rid of him. I can tell he is trying to stay awake, afraid I will hurt him, but it doesn't take long before he is asleep.

Finally, I close my eyes. It is dark when we wake up and the cows are lowing to be milked. The barn door opens and the tavern owner enters carrying a tray laden with food. There is chicken, noodles, and hallah. For a terrible moment my stomach twists and my eyes fill with tears. It is the Sabbath. All the memories of Shabbes flood into me: sitting at the head of my sister's table, eating her food, praying all day in the synagogue. I didn't even realize that it is Friday night.

I shake my head and try to compose myself. I glance at the others. That baby, Samuel, is going to give us all away. I notice that he too wears a cross but tears are streaming down his face.

"Just leave this," I say, making my voice as curt as possible. "We'll be on our way soon."

"But," the innkeeper says timidly, "the cows . . . The neighbors will wonder why they are lowing."

"Milk the cows," Josef says. "And get us some help to saddle the horses."

I see Aaron and Samuel look at Josef, shock in their faces. Of course the innkeeper must milk his cows even on Shabbes or they will suffer. But by demanding he help us with the horses he is forcing a Jew to work on the Sabbath. At least Josef has some guts, unlike those other two. I could like this fellow, I think, if we had met in a different way.

The tavern keeper hurries away. He returns with his sons and they help us with the horses. We gobble down the food, and I can't help but enjoy it.

Finally the horses are ready. We lead them out of the barn. The tavern keeper shows us the road that winds around the town, no more than a dirt trail really. Still, we don't want to ride through town, drawing attention to ourselves. Aaron pays him and he seems happy.

Aaron and Samuel somehow manage to get on their horses. They are pathetic. And that Samuel, his eyes glitter, his brow is damp, he must be sick. I don't think he'll last long.

Josef leads the way, and again I bring up the rear. We walk our horses slowly past the town, fearful of anyone noticing us. The weather has warmed. The unusual cold is leaving. The sky is partly covered with clouds, but the moon is rising and the light will be good. When a cloud covers the moon we can see little, for most of the snow must have melted during the day.

Aaron says we are not far from the frontier. We should reach it sometime during the night if we can travel at a steady pace. We will have to join up with the main road, and when we see the checkpoint we will sneak across the field.

We plod past the town and on into the night. All is quiet. The army may be out looking for us but I don't think our host gave us away. I hear no sounds of hooves beating the ground. I'm sure the army doesn't care much about us, but they must be really mad about their horses. A new recruit tried to escape shortly after I was captured. They flogged him, fifty strokes with the rod. He tried again. He was flogged again. The third time he tried he was made to run the gauntlet. Running down a double line of a hundred men and boys each armed with rods. But many of the other little Jews wouldn't hit him, so they were beaten. Each time he ran away he had been caught by his own squad, who were very careful not to let anyone escape because if they did, they themselves would be flogged. How many were being punished now for our escape, I wonder? Well, I don't really care. Every man for himself, I say.

We join up to the main road now, and Josef tries to get his horse to move faster. The warm air is making the road soft. By tomorrow it'll be in its usual state, thick mud. Still we make good time and we ride steadily without a break. Samuel, in front of me, keeps swaying in his saddle. I wonder whether he'll just fall off and die. We travel for hours, and finally Josef slows his horse.

"I think I see lights ahead," he says. "Let's dismount and take our horses into the fields. I'll go by foot and see if it is the frontier. If it is, we can travel over the fields and just slip across."

They must be gloating about how easy this is

going. But not for long. Not for long. I wait with Aaron and Samuel for Josef to return. They stand together, whispering. I lean against my horse. Finally Josef returns.

"It is a checkpoint," he reports. "We can cross over soon!"

I can hear the excitement in his voice. Now I have to think fast. How do I separate Aaron from the rest? How do I get my revenge, and justice for God? Aaron's horse stamps impatiently. It is a nervous beast and it is a miracle that nothing has happened to Aaron yet, while riding. Not yet. I almost laugh aloud. Of course. It's so simple.

We pull our horses through the fields, which are all plowed under and covered in a thin layer of snow. The horses pick their way through the ruts. We walk for about half an hour and then turn toward the frontier, which must be about fifteen minutes away, on horseback. I have been scanning the fields; now I see what I'm looking for. A small trail, heading right through the fields toward the border.

"Look over there," I say. "We can ride and get there faster."

I don't give them time to think. Instead I mount my horse and wait. They are all behind me. Once they are mounted I start to maneuver my horse past them as if to go to the end of the line, where I usually ride. I pass Josef and then Samuel. When I reach Aaron's horse, before he can react I lean over and grab his horse's reins. With a strong tug I pull them from Aaron's hands and begin to turn the horse around.

"Hey!" he protests. "What are you—"

That's the last I hear from him. Quickly I jump from my horse, holding on to his bit so he doesn't bolt, then I kick Aaron's horse in the side, then in the rump as hard as I can. It rears up, gives a terrified whinny, and bolts across the field, away from the frontier, into the darkness.

"You bastard!" I hear Josef say.

I laugh. He can call me what he wants. The horse and Aaron will soon be sprawled in a muddy rut somewhere and I will be across the border.

I leap onto my horse, wheel around and kick him. Before Josef can stop me I am past him and heading for the frontier. I turn and look. I see them turn their horses and head off after Aaron. Within moments I will be free, and he will be dead, or injured. I hear a scream. Even better! Maybe the border guards will hear and he and his friends will be captured! I lean low over my horse, pat him, and gallop to freedom and a new life. I will head down to a port city and get passage on a ship by offering to work. Maybe I'll go to France, then England. I have to stop myself from screaming with joy. Aaron Churchinsky, I am free of you forever!

CHAPTER 13

Aaron

He has done it before I can react. The horse won't stop and neither does the terror I feel. Somehow I manage to hang on. The horse gallops through the field, never falling, sometimes stumbling, then righting himself. I can hear Josef and Samuel behind me now, but I know they'll never be able to keep up. The horse goes on and on. Through the fear I begin to realize that if the horse doesn't stop, I'll end up back in the town I've just left. I have no reins. I have to throw myself forward, grab his mane with one hand, the saddle with the other, and hold on. I don't know what makes him fall finally. Just a particularly deep rut I think. His front legs buckle beneath him and I fly off, over his head, into the dirt. And then everything goes black.

When I finally wake I feel nothing. I am afraid to

move. Afraid of the pain, or even worse, the absence of pain. Perhaps my back is broken and that is why I feel no pain.

Zev. I'd been so careful, not letting him near me, not trusting him, trying to work out a way to be rid of him, and then with one kick of his boot, one final act of malice, he's ruined all our hopes. I lie on the ground unable to move and I can feel tears on my cheeks. We were so close.

I decide to try wiggling my fingers. Much to my shock I find I can move them. I wiggle first the left hand, then the right. I try to move my toes. I can feel them! Gently I try to raise my head. The pain is excruciating and with a moan I sink back into the ground.

What was that? It's a voice. I'm sure I heard something.

"Aaron, Aaron, are you there?"

It's Samuel.

"His horse is here, he can't be far away."

That's Josef.

Will I be able to speak? I have to try. I open my mouth and try to force some breath out.

"I'm here." It's barely a croak.

"Over there," Samuel says.

Soon they are kneeling by my side.

"Are you hurt?" Samuel asks.

Josef puts his hand to my head, then wipes it on his coat. Is that my blood?

"I don't know," I whisper. "My head hurts."

"Can you move?" Josef asks.

"Don't know," I whisper.

"Try," he says.

I try to move my legs. They respond. Then my arms. I can move them too.

"Good," Josef says, "now we'll try to sit you up." They reach behind me and gently lift me into a sitting position. My head swims and throbs and I feel like I'm going to fall over.

"No, Aaron, stay awake," Josef says. "You're going to be all right. You have a bad cut on your head." He opens his coat, rips off a piece of his shirt, and ties it tight around my head.

"Try to stand. You'll have to ride on the back of my horse."

They help me up. I stagger, unable to keep my balance. I thank God I'm still alive.

"Zev?" I say.

"Gone," Josef mutters. "Probably safely across the border by now. And us, we're almost back to the town we just left. I think we should try to return to that tavern before it gets light. We'll ask him to put us up for one more day. We'll demand it. He won't dare refuse. If you're well enough we'll try again tomorrow."

"My horse?"

"Dead," Josef says. "Come. We can use some money to buy a new one."

Josef mounts his horse. He pulls and Samuel pushes; somehow they get me on. I put my arms around Josef's waist and lean my head against the rough fabric of his coat. Slowly the horse picks his way through the dark until we find the road. The moon is out now and we travel at a quick trot back to town. Every time the horse moves, my body and head feel a terrible jolt. The pain is so severe I know I am weeping. I cannot help it. My left ear feels soaking wet.

"You must have been lying there a long time," Josef says to me. "We had to follow very slowly so as not to hurt the horses."

"I think I was unconscious most of it," I reply through gritted teeth. "I awoke shortly before you arrived."

I rest my head against Josef's back, close my eyes, and try to survive. I slip into a kind of dream, neither waking nor sleeping. I see my mother; she is scolding me for falling off the horse. She has a terrible temper. Her hair is falling out of her scarf, flying about her beautiful face, her black eyes are blazing. My father tries to calm her. He tells her it isn't my fault. All my older sisters, married now, gather around me, fussing over me as they always did, kissing me. Miriam is soothing my head with towels of cool water.

"Gently now, gently," I hear them say.

I open my eyes. Josef and Samuel are carrying me into the barn. It is light enough to see now. The tavern keeper is milking his cows. He gets up in a fright, knocking over the pail.

"What? What?" he says.

"He's been hurt," Josef says. "Can your wife help him?"

The tavern keeper comes over. He looks at my head. He looks at Josef. At Samuel.

"Enough of this nonsense," he says in Yiddish. "You're no more Russian than I am!"

Josef opens his mouth to protest. The man holds up his hand.

"Had I wanted to I would have given you away last night. You're Jewish boys and you're escaping. I'm not a fool. My wife and I discussed it and we decided to protect you. I'll go and get her. That wound looks very bad."

When he leaves Josef starts to laugh. "We may as well have told the truth from the beginning. I don't suppose we'd fool many people."

Even Samuel smiles. "We fooled ourselves into believing we could fool them."

That makes Josef laugh even more.

"Shhh! Do you want to alert the entire town?" The tavern keeper's wife bustles in. "I am Sarah," she says. "This is my husband Mordechai. It's the Sabbath you know," she says, shaking her head. "But God will forgive us. Life before death, even on the Sabbath." She has brought a pail of water, a cloth, and a sewing kit.

She bathes the wound.

"You have a big cut from your forehead to your ear," she says. "It's still bleeding badly. I'll have to sew it up."

"Drink this," says Mordechai. He lifts my head and forces a large mouthful of schnapps down my throat. It makes me cough, which makes my head hurt more. But then I can feel it warming my blood and I lie back in the straw.

Sarah threads the needle and begins to sew up my forehead. Josef and Mordechai hold me down so I don't jump or jar her. Mordechai gives me another schnapps. I sink into the pain, then sink away back to my family and my own room. My mother pulls a warm goose quilt over my body. I nestle into it and sleep.

When I awaken my head is still pounding, but my thoughts are clear and I no longer feel as though I am in some strange dream. I turn my head. Samuel is asleep beside me. I realize immediately how very sick he is. He is pale and his skin is stretched tight over his cheekbones. His breathing is shallow and quick. Josef lies on the other side of me, snoring contentedly.

I close my eyes and fall back to sleep.

I am awakened next by a soft nudge on my shoulder. My eyes fly open, I fear danger. But no, it is Sarah. She carries a candle, as it is dark now. She holds it up to my head.

"Good," she says. "You'll heal nicely, I hope. How do you feel?"

"Hungry," I reply.

"Your friend," she whispers, nodding at Samuel, "he's very sick. He lives in a town only a few miles from yours, he told us before he fell asleep. You should take him home, to his family."

"But how?" I say to her, thinking there is as much

chance of doing that as there is for the sun to rise at night.

"We have a little plan," she confides with a wink. "A good little plan. Wake your friends. Mordechai will come with some food."

I wake up Josef and Samuel. Samuel is shivering and he can't stop. Mordechai comes into the barn with hot chicken soup and bread. We eat, thankful for every mouthful. Samuel at least manages to sip the broth.

Mordechai eyes the crosses at our necks. He sighs. "My sons have been spared only because I pay," he says, "but it costs more and more each year. Now listen. I think I have a plan which will help us all." He pauses. "Your horses," he says, "they are of good stock, worth lots of money, yes?"

"Yes," Josef replies.

"Fine. You give them to me. I sell them. I make enough money to keep my family out of the army for years to come. In the meantime, I have a friend, a clothes merchant who travels to Odessa every year. I will pay him and you will also pay him to take you in his cart. He will drop this one, Samuel, off at his town, then take you both into Odessa. Josef will have to go with you, Aaron. His town is too far away to try to reach safely."

"But how can we return?" I ask. "The kahal knows us. They also know we are supposed to be in the army."

"It will not be an open cart!" Mordechai replies. "You will hide. Samuel must return home."

"If I am to die," Samuel says suddenly, "I would wish to be with my family."

"I think they will bring you back to life, my friend," I say to him. "I think all you need to cure you is their love. They can hide you until you are strong. Then you must come to us in Odessa. We will all have to escape but we will stick together. Josef and I will wait for you."

"It's no worse than the plan which got us here." Josef smiles. "Maybe better. I think it safer than trying to cross the frontier like we did last night. We have no idea what kind of trap Zev could have set for us there. Perhaps somehow he's alerted guards without endangering himself. Or they have found the dead horse and are looking for us. Also, I think this is the only hope for Samuel."

"It's a good plan, Mordechai," I say. "But how will you sell the horses without arousing suspicion?"

"Don't worry." He smiles. "There are ways to get rid of stolen goods and I know them. Rest here tonight," he says. "You will start tomorrow before the sun rises. You will have to ride for eight days lying at the bottom of the cart. We will give you food enough to last you for the journey."

"Just eight days!" I exclaim. "We couldn't be that close to Odessa. We have marched for weeks!" How could I be so close to everything I love and yet have moved so far away from my own self, in such a short time?

"Marching with a group of ragged weak boys is much slower than driving in a cart. Eight days.

That's all. You will get out of the cart only to do what must be done, otherwise you will remain hidden, always. Now rest. I will see you in the morning. Oh, yes, let's get rid of these." And quickly he takes the crosses from around our necks and leaves the barn. Can he also take away the sin we committed by allowing them to be put there in the first place?

I lie back down in the soft hay and let the pounding in my head push me back into a half sleep. But now the image of Zev keeps leaping before my eyes. How could he do it? How could he be the way he is? How could he be so evil? Then I think back to all the things I'd seen since being captured, to the brutality I'd witnessed, and I realize that there are many Zevs in this world. Perhaps he would have been just a town bully, a slightly unpleasant person at worst, if it hadn't been for the czar and his policies of conscription. But the world around him said, Be this, be as bad as you want, and we'll even help you to do it. The world also said that to the sergeants who tortured us to get us to convert. And so the evil that was in them grew and blossomed, watered by the czar and his government. Perhaps, had the kahal not needed kidnappers, Zev would have grown differently, been a different person.

This line of thought confuses me. Does that mean Zev is not to blame for what he did? I try to think clearly. No, no, it cannot be that. He chose to become a khapper. He chose to kick my horse. Oh, yes, I think, I will blame him. I will not forgive him. But I will not forgive the czar either. Or the kahal, because they helped him become what he is.

And me, what have I become? I know now that I, too, have a dark side. And yet, perhaps I need not despise myself for that. Perhaps that too is the fault of the czar and the system that rules us. Or, that system brought out my dark side. Maybe I *should* forgive myself—and maybe it is better not to be deluded, to know everything that is inside. But what a terrible way to learn to understand oneself! Still, I can never go back to the innocent state I lived in before I was captured. I can never go back. Do I dare show this new person to my parents, to Miriam? Won't they find me disgusting, or even worse, won't they be disappointed to discover I am just ordinary, not a brilliant student with all the right answers, just a boy full of weaknesses and doubts. Slowly my eyes begin to close. Tears well up. I was afraid when I was captured and now that I may be going home—I am afraid again.

CHAPTER
14

Aaron

The journey is one long stretch of tedium interspersed with moments of terror. We lie on the bottom of the cart loosely covered by clothes. If the road is clear, we push the clothes aside so we can look up into the sky. When we pass other carts or riders we cover ourselves and allow no movement. On the second day we passed a search party. They stopped Lev, our driver, and asked him if he'd seen four young soldiers on horseback. He shook his head and shrugged. For one moment I was terrified they were going to search the cart.

"Something to buy, officers?" he had said. "Come and look. I have beautiful cloth for you to send home to your wives."

"No, no," they said, no longer interested in the cart, only anxious to get away, to find us, to punish us. I know how the army works. If they cannot find us, they themselves will be punished, flogged and beaten before the men. No one must be allowed to escape without someone suffering the consequences. We heard them ride off and we let out huge sighs. I realized that all of us had been holding our breath.

It is the beginning of the eighth day now. We will soon be in Samuel's town. He is growing weaker by the moment and I pray his family can help him. I am worried though. I had promised him we would wait, but he is so weak it could be a month before he is ready to travel. And it will be almost impossible for our families to hide us for a month. We must leave Odessa soon. We must leave Russia. Every moment we spend on Russian soil is an added danger to our lives.

He coughs constantly, and his fever is high. Still, one can recover from a fever. As long as it is not cholera or typhoid, he may live. I want him to live so badly. I do not want them to defeat him.

As if reading my thoughts he says to me, "You must not wait for me. I will only slow you down. You and Josef must escape. Somehow I will join you, when I'm stronger. Just tell me how to contact your family and I will follow."

I tell him where my family lives and I tell him where Miriam lives. I don't argue with him because I know it is fruitless.

"Cover up!" Lev shouts to us.

We do.

"I can smell my town," Samuel says. "I know we have arrived."

He grasps my hand and holds on tight. He is overcome with emotion at the thought of seeing his parents and his family.

"I have to thank you, Aaron," he whispers. "You convinced me to live. You have brought me here. God bless you."

I squeeze his hand.

"Don't give up now," I admonish him. "The fight for a new life is just beginning."

After a while the wagon stops. I hear Lev go from the wagon, knock on a door. I hear a small cry, a woman's cry, then voices shushing her.

Lev's voice is suddenly very close.

"All right, Samuel, there's no one on the street. Come out now and hurry straight into the house."

Samuel throws the clothes back and scrambles out of the wagon. Within seconds the door is shut, but I can hear muffled weeping and cries of joy.

"I don't think we'll ever see him again," Josef says. "But at least he'll die with his family."

"Don't say that," I say. "You'll make it happen. Of course we'll see him. The three of us will go to England and he'll become a great scholar. You'll see."

Suddenly I am afraid that the angel of death will hear Josef and run after Samuel. I had always laughed at my mother when she'd suggested such things, but now it doesn't seem so silly. I feel that he is hovering near us, waiting, waiting.

The next few hours I spend in a state of excruciating expectation. I picture the scene over and over in my mind. Myself in my mother's arms, my father hugging me and crying, my sisters being told as they come from their homes, one by one. And of course, Miriam. I long for her so much it hurts, a pain almost unbearable. I picture our house, the wooden floors, the kitchen always filled with the smell of fresh bread, soup, meat. My little alcove in the other room, filled with books, my little bed, and my own goose quilt. How happy I was.

It is night when we arrive in Odessa. The streets are quiet. Finally the wagon stops.

"This must be it," Lev says. "I'll go and see."

My heart pounds so, I get it confused with the sound of him knocking on the door.

I hear his voice, speaking low, and then I hear my mother's voice. I can hear the shock, the disbelief in the tone, even though I can't make out the words.

"Come, boys," Lev whispers.

We throw the clothes off and rush off of the wagon. We race for the door. But is it my mother standing there in the doorway, the light behind her? I reach the door. She pulls us all in and shuts it behind her. Then she folds me in her arms. I push her back and look again. It is her but what has happened to her? She looks old! Tears flow down her face. She gazes at me and notices my dismay.

"Oh," she says, "it doesn't matter." And she hugs me again.

"I must go," Lev says. "Good luck, boys. May God be with you."

Josef and I shake his hand and thank him warmly. We have already paid him and he has left the money at home with his wife—just in case we were all captured.

"Mama," I say when he leaves, "this is my friend Josef."

She takes his hands in hers. Then she drops them and holds my hands. She looks at me. She seems unable to speak or move.

"Mama," I ask, "where is Papa?"

"Papa?" she asks, as if for a moment she can't imagine who I mean. "Oh, Papa! He is at a client's house. He will be back soon."

Finally she seems to pull herself together. "You will both come with me to the kitchen and you will eat and you will tell me everything. Every *single* thing."

She feeds us bread and soup and noodles and meat. It is so wonderful I can hardly stand it. Between mouthfuls I tell her of my capture and of our escape. But how much dare I tell her? That I converted? The horrors I experienced? I only tell her the bare facts, for now. Then she lets us go to the outhouse in the back. When we return we see she has filled the bathtub with steaming water.

"I will lay fresh sleeping clothes out on your bed, Aaron. Josef may sleep on a mat beside you. I will wait in the sitting room for Papa. Tomorrow we will figure something out."

I could see the old fire in her eyes. "Don't worry. They won't catch you again. And although I curse Zev Lobonsky, I thank him too, for sending you back to me. Now I can say good-bye and I know you will be safe. I know it."

I am not as confident as she is, but I try not to think about it. For now I enjoy the moments as they come. I wash, I clean my hair, I scrub myself until my skin hurts. I settle Josef in the pallet on the floor, and then I go to my bed. I can see the pain in Josef's eyes. He may never see his family again. But he can write them once we are free, and at least they will know he is safe. That will mean everything to them. Mother has put a hot brick at the bottom of the bed for my feet. I pull the goose quilt up around my shoulders. Now I am happy. Completely happy. I close my eyes and sleep.

I think my father comes into the room at some point in the night. I feel his hand on my cheek but I am too deep in sleep to really wake up. But when I open my eyes in the morning, he is there sitting on my bed, staring at me.

"Papa!" I shout and fling my arms around him.

"Aaron," he šays, and he starts to weep. Quickly he brushes the tears away. "Come, we have no time for tears. Get dressed. Warm clothes. Layers. I have a plan but it must be done today. First go to the kitchen, someone is waiting for you."

Somehow I had hoped they would hide me here, that I would not have to go away again.

I hurry. My whole body is trembling. I know

who waits for me in the kitchen. I pause for a moment before entering, then take a deep breath and walk in.

Miriam sits in a chair facing the door. Her brown eyes are moist with tears, her cheeks are pale. She tries to get up but doesn't seem to have the strength. I move over to her. Kneel.

"Aaron," she whispers, "I never gave up hope."

I smile at her. She leaps from her chair and throws herself into my arms. I know it is wrong to embrace her like this before we are married but I also no longer think God punishes us for such small transgressions. No, I think the rules are far different from that. We kiss. Never have I been so happy. I want the moment to last forever.

Her knees buckle under her and I have to help her back into the chair. Once again I kneel by her. We hold hands and gaze into each other's eyes.

She rouses herself to speak. And when she speaks she smiles that wonderful, radiant smile of hers. "Your father has told me his plan," she says. "It is a good one. I want you to know that when you can send for me, I will come. I can easily get papers. I want to leave. I want to be with you."

And now I know I have to say something. I must tell her the truth. "Miriam," I say, "you must not be so hasty and say you will follow me. I am no longer the person you once knew. I—I—Miriam, I converted. Until a few days ago I wore a cross around my neck. I wanted to kill Zev I hated him so much. I have so much hate and anger in me. I'm not worthy of you anymore. And I don't know what I'll do with my life. I still want to study but, Miriam, it can never be the same! I can never be the same!"

For a minute Miriam doesn't speak. When she does I am shocked. "I'm glad you are no longer perfect, Aaron. It is the one thing that worried me about our marriage. Because I am *so* imperfect. You are human, that is all. You say you wanted to kill Zev. But you didn't, did you? To have those feelings, that is normal, to act on them—that is inexcusable. I love you," she adds simply. "Together we will try to understand what this life is all about."

Just then my father comes to the door. "Come, children," he says, "we haven't much time. Come into the other room." We follow him.

Josef is there already and so are all my sisters and their husbands. No children except babies who cannot tell tales. Everyone fusses over me, kisses me. Even Josef gets hugged and kissed, much to his embarrassment.

Josef and I eat hot cereal, sweet rolls and drink tea. Finally my father tells everyone they must go. No one is to know the escape plan but us, then nothing can go wrong. My sisters are insulted, protesting that they won't say a word.

"But if a child overhears," Papa says. "No, we won't risk it. God has given us a chance to say good-bye. We must thank Him for that."

"Do we thank Him for taking Aaron away from us forever too?" Mama says.

No one answers. Everyone hugs me and says

good-bye. Everyone cries. Including me. The hardest part is saying good-bye to Miriam, but she is so strong.

"We won't say good-bye, Aaron. We will see each other again soon, I know we will." And then she turns and hurries out the door. Finally we are just the four of us again.

"There is a ship in the harbor," Papa says. "It is a grain ship. It leaves for France today. I have arranged for you both to be on it. I have spoken to the first mate and I gave him money. He has promised to take you but warns me you'll have to work, scrubbing the decks, things like that."

"Papa," I say, "I have money. Let me give it to you."

"I'll take a little," he says, "but you must keep the rest. You'll need it. I have a good trade here. Mama and I will always get by."

He must have given all his savings to the sailor. I go for my money bag and empty half of it onto the counter.

"We won't need more than this, Papa," I say. "Maybe you and Mama can use this to come and join me in England. Then we can all be together again. And you'll bring Miriam too."

Papa's eyes light up.

"That is a good idea," he says. "A very good idea. The sooner we all leave this country the better. Things can only get worse for the Jews, not better. Now put the rest of the money away, say good-bye to your mother, and let us go."

It's all happening too fast. I say good-bye to Mama in a haze of tears and grief. And then we are hurrying through the streets, caps over our heads, hoping no one will recognize me. Papa does not walk with us. That would certainly draw attention to me. Instead we take parallel streets and meet up again at the harbor. We thread our way through the hustle and chaos until we reach the large cargo ship. Papa tells us to wait. Finally the first mate appears at Papa's side. He looks us over, nods, then motions us up the ramp. I turn to Papa, give him one last hug. Then I walk up the ramp onto the boat, and off Russian soil forever. Josef looks at me. Our eyes meet. In a few hours we will be truly free. We will start a new life in a new land. I want to throw my hat into the air and scream. Instead I grab the mop and follow the first mate into the hold.

Zev and Aaron

PART 1
ZEV

It hasn't been easy but I've made it. I had to travel by night. I've had almost no food and only what I could steal from a well to drink. Finally, yesterday, I sold my horse and was able to buy food and drink. I stand at the harbor watching the ship as it docks. It has come from Odessa and will go on to France. I will stay in France, I think, and get work as a butcher. I am well trained. I'll find work. I'll marry. I'll start my own family. No one will ever know about my life in Russia, what I did, who I was. I'll be a new Zev Lobonsky. The ship docks. When the ramp is down I search out the first mate. He is busy supervising the loading.

"Can you use an extra hand?" I ask.

He looks at me. "Can you pay?" he asks.

I nod. It's crazy to have to bribe them to get on a ship so you can work, but I know this is the easiest way to get to France.

"Well, in that case," he says, "I can. Took some hands on in Odessa, but one of them has spent the whole week too sick to work. Worst case of seasickness I've ever seen. You'll mop and swab and wash down. You'll pay me now and I'll see you get food. Where are you headed?"

"France."

"Let's see your money."

I pay him almost everything I've got, then go up the ramp and onto the ship. Here in Romania no one seems to care that I don't have papers. The only thing they care about is money.

I wait on deck for the first mate. When he gets on board he says to me, "You'll work with the other fellows I hired. They'll show you the routine. Here they come. Listen to that one, Josef, he knows the ropes."

I turn and look. My stomach sinks into my feet. My mouth turns dry. This can't be. It can't be. Josef stands before me, hands on hips. Beside him is Aaron. He looks thin and his face has a green pallor. He must be the one who is seasick. He is so shocked he doesn't react. Neither do I. We are all frozen to the spot.

"You all look like you've seen a ghost," the first mate jokes. "Now there's work to be done, so get to it."

I thought I was free. I thought I could start fresh. I thought that with Aaron dead my past was dead too. But I cannot get rid of him.

"Maybe you'd be safer on another ship," Josef says, very quietly.

"There is no other ship," I reply. "The first mate has all my money. This is my only chance."

"No." Aaron smiles. "Let him stay, Josef. I want him to stay."

I look at Aaron. His smile is peculiar. He means to kill me. I can tell. There are two of them. They can protect each other. But how can I protect myself? He'll kill me in that one moment when I fall asleep, that one moment I'm off my guard.

"He can't stay awake forever." Aaron smiles, as if I am not there.

I spin around and chase after the first mate.

"I've changed my mind," I say. "I want to get off. I want my money back."

"What money?" he says. "I don't have any of your money."

"See those two," I say. "They're my enemies. I can't travel with them. They'll kill me."

He shrugs and walks back down the ramp. I turn and look at Aaron and Josef. I hate them so much. I turn and walk down the ramp. Somewhere in Romania they must need a good butcher. Perhaps I could travel into Austrian territory. There are many big cities there. I'll find work. I'll survive. God, as always, will be with me to show me the way. In fact, God must have put Aaron on this ship for a reason—perhaps I was never meant to go to France. Perhaps this ship will sink and Aaron will go down with it.

I look back over my shoulder. Aaron and Josef are staring at me. Josef spits on the floor in disgust. Aaron just stares. He would have killed me. I know it. Well, he won't get the chance.

Once again he's wrecked my plans. Always, always, he ruins things for me.

If it wasn't for him, I think, my life would have been perfect. If it wasn't for him. He will stick in my heart always, like an illness I can't rid myself of. I curse him as I turn and walk away.

PART 2
AARON

As I stand and stare at Zev, the cause of all my misery, I still want to kill him. I will plan it, detail by detail. He will be so tired after the backbreaking work, he will have to sleep and then I will take his neck in my bare hands and I will strangle him. Because he deserves no better. And so I say to Josef, a smile on my face, "He can't stay awake forever. Josef, we can take turns sleeping." I say this to Josef since I could not bear to actually speak to Zev.

Then I see the fear in Zev's eyes. And the hate. And suddenly all the hate I feel drains out of my body and my head and my heart, and instead all I feel is pity. I know that I won't kill him. I am about to tell him so but at that moment he turns and walks away.

As his back recedes into the milling crowds of people on the deck I feel a huge weight lift from my heart. I do not want to spend the rest of my life filled with hate, rage, and thoughts of revenge. I realize suddenly that he can only ruin my life if I allow him to do so. And I will not. He is a poor soul who must live constantly tortured with dark thoughts. I will not let him turn me into that. It would be his final triumph. I will survive. I'll see my family again. I'll see Miriam again. We'll start fresh in a better place.

I feel around my neck, just to be certain that the hated cross is really gone. It is, of course, but the confusion of the last few weeks remains very much with me. I will be able to start fresh with everything but not with God; I have a lot of thinking to do about God. Of course I renounce my conversion. I will always be a Jew. I want to study more. I still hope Samuel will join us, and the three of us will be together again. How I envy Josef and Samuel. Josef knows there is no God, Samuel believes with certainty that there is and that he knows what God wants of him. And me? I have questions, only questions, no answers. Except one. I know it is better to have love in my heart than hate. So if there is a God, I thank Him for Miriam—without her I would know only anger and bitterness.

I turn to my best friend. Josef smiles at me and slaps me on the back.

I take a deep breath of fresh air and watch Zev Lobonsky disappear from my life and from my heart forever. The future holds nothing but uncertainty for me, yet perhaps that is the true state of life—and I rejoice at the adventure that lies ahead.

You'll want to read these
compelling, hard-hitting novels by

Bette Greene